18 7   99

CW01512119

The Reali

The Reality Factor

Mark King

The Pentland Press Limited
Edinburgh • Cambridge • Durham • USA

First published in 1996 by
The Pentland Press Ltd.
1 Hutton Close
South Church
Bishop Auckland
Durham

British Library Cataloguing in Publication Data.
A Catalogue record for this book is available
from the British Library.

ISBN 1 85821 406 8

Typeset by CBS, Felixstowe, Suffolk
Printed and bound by Antony Rowe Ltd., Chippenham

Chapter One

Bob Driscoll couldn't believe it, his eyes stared down at the print: 'One in every five men is a bisexual'. His eyelids fluttered betraying any pretence of credibility, for he could have sworn that the ratio was only one in every twelve. Still – he fully realised that it was only a cheap tabloid he'd happened to read, one of superficial titillation, and besides, statistics could mean virtually anything. His eyes surveyed the smoky café, a snug little place which he'd frequented over the years, then his eyes came to rest, to a thoughtful focus, on a vision of an enigma. Or at least it was an enigma to Bob Driscoll, this dark napolitan mystery upon which his gaze was hopelessly held captive.

It was really weird, so strange. For in many ways his wife was far prettier, much more chatty, a good deal less impersonal or cold even. Yet for some elusive reason, Miss Carrero was a thousand times more seductive than Bob's own wife could ever be. Miss Carrero could melt any 'macho' defence of pretended disinterest or disinclination without her even taking off any of her clothes. It was those beguiling eyes that burned into your loins, that darkness of skin with her jet black hair carelessly tussled into an erotic naturalness that evoked raw passion in her many helpless male victims. When she strutted across the café she owned, her curvature played hell with Bob's hormones, sent any sense of reserve or composure utterly haywire. And she knew it. But crucially there was one thing she didn't know, and that was that although Doctor Bob Driscoll was fascinated by

1

her, somebody else enchanted him even more, and it wasn't his wife. It was Daniel Broughton. This slim, often giggly nineteen-year-old of the same sex was, above all, Bob's most hallowed, treasured prize. A patient too – one with a mental illness, one with a very long history of institutional care. Often prone also to suicidal attempts, hysterical outburst, sometimes un-predictable aggression towards hospital staff. Yet still Bob loved him, unknown to Bob's wife, unknown to Miss Carrero. That was Bob's biggest secret, one which, if broadcasted to anyone, would be one huge shocking surprise, yet so far totally undisclosed.

Such was the convoluted complexity of sex, its strangeness; it could be an erotic oven of crazy desire or a refrigerator of cold rejection. Was the way that woman carefully bagged up coins into small plastic holders in any way predictable? Could you predict whether it would take a matter of minutes or many years to gain and keep Miss Carrero's trust, or love? Bob couldn't, certainly not with her as he watched a feminine potential millionaire in the making. He wondered where she lived, what she did in her leisure time – if she had any, that was. But money was at least no headache for her, the ruby earrings studded into her fleshy brown lobes was ample testimony to comfortable wealth. In a rather weird way he started to feel a little sorry for her, convinced she didn't have fun. Or was that a totally incorrect way of thinking to hide his miserable plight of late? Namely, that it wasn't Miss Carrero he was sorry for at all, but himself – because it was he – Doctor Bob Driscoll, overworked, strained, and drained – who was missing out on fun. Above all, the most worrying thought for Doctor Driscoll was his painful awareness of his own insecurity – and its transference upon his Italian feminine victim. His stomach curdled at his acute realization of her current success and his current failure, her wins, his losses. It made him not only ashamed to realize he could do such a thing, but angry that he, as an eminent psychiatrist, should be thinking in such a bitter, twisted way. He needed to get away from the café, its company, the burger smell, the greasy tables and hard uncomfortable seats. Without meeting Miss Carrero's eyes he thrust a couple of notes into her hand and muttered somewhat incoherently 'Goodnight.' She then, as she always had done for over five years, replied with the same words in the same tone 'Goodnight sir,' as Doctor Bob Driscoll, tired and maybe a bit confused, walked out into the November chill.

Perhaps he'd drank too much coffee - he needed the toilets. It was always so extremely annoying that most modernized cities had so few public toilets. But Bob knew of some archaic ones, almost ancient in stench of putrefaction, ones where you descend slippery steps, hence these bogs were underground. It was a long time since he'd last been to them, these secret testimonies to a thousand implicit undercover, gay encounters, although that was not his current preoccupation. They loomed up in misty murkiness and he carefully descended to fall victim to an olfactory assault of a violent reek of bleach. There was nobody else there. He was greatly relieved that inner city demolition and the monster of modern architecture had as yet not removed the place, denied naturalistic needs. Clouds of blue smoke came from his cigarette, temporarily suspended in the dark, damp air, as he threw it away, only half-finished.

It was like a tomb, almost a surrealistic setting, the poor electric lighting revealing sepulchral stalls, these shrouded amongst black sinks and mucky tiles. It was as if every single piece of anything pot or ceramic was cracked, semi-shining in a grubbiness, a wetness. His eyes allowed him to make a rather strange assessment, comparisons with previous visitations. For straightaway he was able to identify what was, and what was not, familiar. Whereas there always used to be three cubicles now, there was only one. That solitary remaining cubicle brought a resounding jolt of memory flooding back, a jarring reminder of his first encounter with Daniel Broughton, maybe five, even six years ago. The act. The unpublicised, undisclosed, undercover act, buried in history, but so very excitingly preserved in Bob's bedtime memory, a nice thought at night.

So much a defunct part of the past, but needing phoenix qualities, requiring an occurrence, a rebirth again. Such thoughts made instant jelly of his loins, thoughts passionately rushing back. Daniel now hospitalized in a psychiatric ward of Rosedale, no longer an academic student, and his doctor, by weird coincidence, turning out to be Bob Driscoll.

He lit another cigarette praying to fate that the past could return, if not immediately, then very soon. He couldn't stand sensuous deprivation, sexual denial; he felt such a loss that if it continued, it would kill him. He'd definitely see Daniel tomorrow, take him for a long stroll in the Rosedale grounds, have coffee, smoke, laugh and joke, enjoyably live and love. Life wasn't about working or marriage - just about seizing opportunities of chance, which if you didn't grab them fast then you lost them forever; they just died. Daniel Broughton was a massive chance, an opportunity never to be allowed to be missed, something for Bob far greater than God, never to fade, perish. For Bob Driscoll, Daniel was everything; the universe.

But the suffocating dampness was getting to him, the stifling drip, drip, drip, from ceiling to small puddles on the floor. He made up his mind never ever to come to these same toilets again; it was all played out. As he climbed the green steps it felt good to breathe real air again in contrast to minutes spent in the nostalgic stench. He made for his nearby maroon Jag. Once inside he brought the motor into life, growling like a baby dinosaur. It was a beautiful leathery cocoon and the leather seats smelt good and felt soft as he switched on the internal demister system. He inserted a jazz cassette tape and accelerated into the night.

Such warmth and security of Driscoll's Jaguar was something Daniel Broughton would have given anything for as he writhed in the turmoil of an uneasy vicious sleep. November's coldness was creeping through the wooden window-panes of Rosedale's dormitories, its frozen breath upon the patients, those compulsory clients of Rosedale judged to be of unsound mind.

Rosedale: a psychiatric sprawling mass of red-bricked testimony to the Victorian zeal of asylum building. The legacy of how the awkward nineteenth century question of what to do with society's nonconformists was custodially and cruelly answered – namely to lock them up. The Victorian era had little room for those whom it saw as of poor constitution or of feeble mind. Best, then, to let Great Britain progress materially without disruption from those classed as loonies; simply lock them up.

'Out of sight out of mind', this still quite prominent in Rosedale, despite vociferous official claims to the contrary. So little altered, so little changed. For anyone labelled as economically unproductive, either a century ago or now was not to be tolerated out on the city streets but compulsorily confined due to being 'mentally unwell'. An untarnished, unaltered photograph a hundred years on from the early asylum to the glittering mental hospital innovations of the present with exactly the same 'solution' to the same perceived problem.

Was it all actually, tangibly, factually real – all of this – the hell, the utter unfairness, the pain? Certainly to Daniel's mind, his way of nocturnal thought, it was all too horribly real. How his mind could torture his own body of flesh, nerves and bone is a very difficult question; but as any psychiatrist knows, hallucinatory and delusional states are every bit as real to the sufferer as to anything of 'normal' sensation, to somebody not so unfortunately inflicted.

Still no deliverance from his hallucinatory evil – despite his time-worn reiterated prayer: 'Forgive us our trespasses'; – he asked himself what trespass had he supposedly done to deserve this plight? Daniel was no criminal, hadn't wished, requested, consciously volunteered to contract a psychiatric illness. Where, he often weepingly thought, is the supposed justice or fairness in this world? To realise there was so often none only served to compound his agony, his suffering – usually to suffer by day, but to be plagued a thousand times worse by way of nocturnal psychotic symptoms at night. How he wished he might be a victim of sleeplessness, for insomnia would remove his nightly plunge into his mentally created hell.

His head inside was spinning in sickening delirium as his twitching face indicated that the dormitory chill had succeeded in defeating his sleep; he was coming round to wakefulness – a massively desired one at that. Upwards from the iron bedstead were the familiar, red ragged dormitory curtains and a moth fluttering about crazily colliding with the dim dormitory electric light. His entire body was sweat-soaked, saturated as a consequence of an illness many people knew he undoubtedly had, but only he knew its hideous intensity, its vilest of sensations. Such unreality was, for Daniel Broughton, only too terrifyingly real.

But for Bob, rocketing through the filthy weather, there was a different kind of blackness. He was dying to close his eyelids as the monotony of windscreen wipers lulled him almost as if by hypnosis into lethargy. This was a familiar drive – back home. But home to what? To talk about a job no longer attractive, a meaningless mid-forties watershed of despair, a disillusioning crossroads? He was facing a job he'd started to hate, a wife he no longer loved, a home he rarely lived in: just a greyness of a much dreaded future.

If the clouds would only mercifully clear to reveal some kind of picture, a map of one's position within the boundaries of destiny. Even bleak, bad news of a future would be better than no news at all; that's the sickener, he resignedly thought, accepting it without anger; just a crushing, cramping sense of helpless loss, as he struggled to open the staid ritual of his rusting green garage doors. Same old doors, same old wife, same old car, same old life.

As the corrugated screech of the doors died away, blowing out cheeks in exhaustion he eased his Jaguar into the garage's dusty mustiness, next to Gill's car. He wasn't particularly hungry, although that would disappoint Gill, as she'd have prepared a good meal. This was revealed by the look on her face as he quietly insisted upon a sandwich and coffee only, nothing else. 'You're sodden, soaked like a whale,' she compassionately said as he rubbed his face, neck and ears on a couple of kitchen cloths. At her genuine concern he brightened a bit saying that if he caught pneumonia he could at least take a rest from being harassed and hassled at Rosedale. 'Probably do us both good,' she exclaimed, 'That job's well nigh destroying us.'

There was no denying it – Gill was a very clever woman. For a split second he felt like telling her everything, removing all his mental clothing of disguise, baring his naked truth, sharing secrets she perhaps knew fully anyway. What a tough, double intricate game or more simply, sad game, of calling her bluff. If only, he thought, he could still love her, but knew it was useless because something had changed – he couldn't be and wasn't the ambitious extrovert of over twenty years ago; life had moulded his plasticine of a personality in drastically different ways. Did she know that? She surely must. Did she twig onto his affair with one of his patients? A male patient, one happening to be psychiatrically ill? No, perhaps not, or at least not yet.

Gill Driscoll had so much more to give her husband than he had to give her. It wasn't a matter of her putting in a great effort, nothing to do with questions of commitment or motivation. It was rather that so far her love for him had not yet fully died. His attraction to Gill had petered out, not through

7

any growing disinterest or repulsiveness of looking at a plainer face growing yet plainer over thousands of bleary-eyed boring breakfasts. Whether or not she was now less pretty, more jaded was not the reason; rather his tragic twist of a bisexual Achilles' heel he often hated but could not relinquish, could only continue pitifully, if pleasurably, to pursue. Certainly she would stick with him through the turmoil of what a life and marriage was supposed to be, what love meant – or was said to be: a joint effort, experience, united endeavour, whatever.

Yet upon Gill, too, it was taking its toll, its strain of her feeling more and more that her husband was almost becoming a stranger. Not significantly any warmer or approachable than the man in blue overalls who occasionally came to fix the blocked waste disposer, or the council worker who did garden repairs of the dilapidated wooden fencing. Crucially both Gill and Bob had enormous reserves of love still to give – but no longer to each other, and this they knew, and most importantly of all – the reason why. For the reason was not increasing sexual indifference, but that Rosedale virus, the career of a cancer eating at him, and that in its turn having bad effects upon her. They both realised that. Another job was however not at all a viable proposition, not a choice he had or could take; his age, his specific skills left him trapped at present as an occupational prisoner in Rosedale. They realised that too. To be quite correct, Bob knew that even Danny Broughton was not the reason – for, as in fact was the case, he could continue to love Daniel and simultaneously placate Gill. That task was not by any means impossible. Difficult perhaps, but not beyond his means. But what was the really deadly opponent was a reluctant location in a mental health service in which over twenty years had stripped his ideas, ambitions of professional autonomy and reduced him to a cog in the wheel status of an amorphous pay-roll employee. A career drained of being able to independently make decisions, choices, a job strangled of a capacity of flexibility, an exodus of options.

Still, it was to no avail; just Bob Driscoll talking to the wind, banging his head against a brick wall. He lay in bed that night feeling like recoiling from her touch. More than anything else at that precise moment he wanted to tell her he loved her. But he could not, would not, tell such a deliberate lie. Her almost sickly, overheated clammy touch, the nausea of undesired, repulsing sex made him feel like vomiting. With great effort he forced himself mechanically to kiss her, then lay back wiping his lips; he would have rather kissed the cold bedroom walls. She had soon after fallen asleep, he looking guiltily at her face, feeling almost as if he was betraying her, that pang of conscience only serving to make him more annoyed with himself and increased the difficulty of getting to sleep.

The electric bedside clock showed three-thirty a.m., as he heard the wind and rain lashing the windows; he reached for some sleeping pills. His thoughts were colliding into a seemingly irresolvable confusion – be they of a ramshackle Rosedale or a fondness for some young man of a gender totally unlike that of Gill. If he could only go back twenty years or so, then he would never, with hindsight, have committed his crime – of marrying someone like her. The crime of injury upon Gill by way of causing her the mental wound of his unreturned love. For it seemed to Bob Driscoll that few crimes are so serious as to tell someone you'll love them forever, only to later capitulate, pull out, quit the venture. This crime he felt he'd deliberately and blatantly done. Once again, there was no cool, soothing balm; no pleasant easy solution to still the hurting, the soreness of one's actions, no matter how deeply one happened to regret them.

And regret them so bitterly, and frustratingly hopelessly, Bob Driscoll so truly, pitifully did.

Chapter Two

Frank Farley, editor of the *Mercury* blew angry smoke-rings up to the nicotine-stained ceiling. His jaw twitched irritably and then he just as irritably, even irascribly, spoke: 'It's a dead cert Jim. If we don't act, don't go in now; if we're not fast, sure hard, if we pussy-foot around, we might as well say goodbye to the best serial story for years.'

'But remember the last time,' said Jim Holland. 'The threat of a legal precedent by the Rosedale top dogs upon us, only us.'

'Yes, yes, yes, I know all that Jim, but it was a bluff, a massive hell of a bluff by Rosedale, a bluff they banked on, couldn't afford to lose. We've got the ace card, they know that; do you see it clear as me, Jim? For God's sake agree! Commit yourself to fact and reason. It's one hell of a story.'

'Who goes in hard then?' asked Holland, knowing the answer to his own question.

'Do I have to really answer that, Jim?' said Farley, flustered and fogged up with too many coffees and cigars.

Jim Holland paused. 'Me, I suppose, or should I automatically assume, of course?'

'Of course!' Farley crackled his grin wide, his yellow broken teeth bared in ugliness, 'That's the only way ahead to get to chief reporter: work, and bloody hard consistent work at that!'

Jim Holland reflectfully tugged his ear lobe. It was a mission with as many potential legal pitfalls giving a danger level he was terrifyingly getting used to. The north face of the newspaper

Eiger, a business which could give you an overnight success story if you got a big swoop right, a good story; but out on the streets if you failed.

'You see,' said Frank, 'the guys I take on, hopefuls like you, have to be like the name of our paper itself – like Mercury – fast, quicksilvers of story finders, precious story sellers. That's why you can get off your backside now, get homing in around loonyland!'

Jim Holland was then destined for that secret red-brick fortress of a secure psychiatric unit – sprawling, elusive, an enigma of an enemy to the tabloid press: Rosedale. If he put just one foot wrong he'd have nothing less than Rosedale's legal specialists prosecuting him, the Home Office breathing down his neck, and the officialdom of the Health Service pressing relentlessly for his imprisonment.

'What a career,' he muttered under his breath as Frank Farley lit another smelly cigar.

Farley blew out the burning match and looked vacantly at Holland, their eyes meeting, both understanding the business of the rest of the afternoon. 'Well then?' said Farley, implying Holland's task and destination.

Jim Holland rose from an uncomfortable swivel chair. 'Yes, Rosedale,' he quietly said.

There were two possible ways to glean long suspected newsworthy material about Rosedale, or for that matter any secure mental institution. Both were difficult, both often failed, culminating in the press being red-faced, apologetic, and hit in the pocket. The first route on such a hazardous mountain, an actual Eiger of obstacles of eager reporters at their peril, was to formally request an interview with personnel. Invariably, this was rejected without any reasons given as to why. With this procedure, people like Frank Farley or Jim Holland, his sidekick, were unhappily very familiar. So they were to try a different tactic, another angle – the just-as-hazardous but potentially-more-

11

hopeful second ploy. It was essentially to try and identify personnel who could be cajoled, even bribed into subversion; a betrayal of secretive data of their own employing organisation. But, Holland wondered, who? Who in that sprawling complex behind great gates of Victorian iron, and a seventeen-foot-high perimeter wall dotted with grotesque gargoyles, would be a potential subversive for disclosure to a paper like the *Mercury*?

Jim Holland drew hard on a cigarette, feeling weak, having been living on a bad diet of chocolate and sandwiches for several hectic days. Then, suddenly, it came to him like a golden glory of an avenue lying ahead of him – his alert, resourceful mind had twigged Rosedale's possible only weakness.

Jim Holland smiled to himself, for Frank would be so bloody proud and pleased at Jim's unique reportage success. Jim, shrewd, now decisive, pointed his feet towards a nearby phone booth with his single undivided focus of determination – to contact direct Rosedale's Social Work Division.

And yet this rope was to break; Holland was to come tumbling down – temporarily at least – his tolerance threshold being strained to the absolute limit due to secret officialdom and red tape. Jim Holland had met an icy, ungiving wall of no compromise. Infuriated by switchboard secretarial bitchiness he fumed at being treated like a little lad in short trousers; some anonymous functionary formally instructing him about 'correct' organisational procedure as regards external enquiries. As he sat back in his *Mercury* stuffy office, he still smarted from the conversational sting. Had he not simply requested to talk to a senior social worker, only to be told that initially a letter in writing would be required? A necessary preliminary to any such desired establishing of contact with Rosedale's Social Work Sector?

Indeed he had tried hard to be nice, polite, reasonable and amenable, only to receive a lecture about administrative 'do's and 'don'ts'. Now he decided that it was time to quit being nice and be nasty instead. He foraged through a mass of clippings – all bits of Rosedale scandals, be they by *Mercury* reporters or other rival papers.

Holland psyched himself up to be unpleasantly ruthless as he scanned clippings over recent Rosedale years. One in particular was interesting. Unfortunately not a *Mercury* original, and only a generalised speculative slur. One and a half million pounds granted from the Health Department to be used for 'Rehabilitative Expansion'. Presumably, Holland thought, it must be for more facilities, maybe more recreational things such as a patients' social club or even a small gymnasium. There again, it could be for something more sensational as regards a story if the cash were for patients' outings, shopping trips into the community; on the streets, patients mingling with the public. That was the kind of line for a good article on page one – Holland could already visualise the caption now: MADMEN LET LOOSE TO ROAM or HORROR ON OUR HIGH STREETS!

But what if the one and a half million had not been used for these purposes, nor even intended to be? In that case it was fertile ground for an even more exciting revelation – one of hospital financial embezzlement. Again titles of a dramatic exposé excitedly loomed up in Holland's mind: PILFERING FROM PATIENTS or THE GREAT ROSEDALE RIP OFF. Things were starting to move for the *Mercury* now, as the wheels of imagination started to move in Jim Holland's head. He might take the *Mercury* to the very top – and most important – *himself* to the top.

Yet so stubbornly the problem remained, namely access to information concealed within, behind that high perimeter wall. What then about a deception strategy, a ploy founded upon a carefully constructed lie? What, for instance, about a bogus identity of an eager, fresh out of college, budding social worker? A suitably qualified ambitious, anxious-to-be humanitarian and whatever else crap that could convince Rosedale's switchboard that a promising social worker wished to be on their pay-roll as an employee? Jim Holland reached for the phone. The phone burring crackled, interrupted by a very cool, laid-back feminine tone of voice. For a full five minutes Jim was, amazingly, able to convincingly tell a fat package of lies so incredibly easily. She'd swallowed it like a helpless hypnotised child would do with favourite sweets. He politely ended the conversation by checking his interview appointment time of ten a.m. in exactly a week's time with a guy called Dave Harrison, Senior Social Worker. He foraged in his pockets for a badly needed cigarette, lit it, sat back, feet on his desk and smiled. Go in hard, lie through the teeth, forget tact, throw morals out of the window; Jim Holland was going to become a good newspaper reporter.

The public view of Rosedale must always be one of a gullible admiration. A hospital that the country would always look up to, be proud of. So it was that, just as Jim Holland was drinking cans of lager in front of his word-processor at home already toying with what he firmly believed would be a national critical exposé of the year, David Harrison was thinking about Jim Holland's planned chat. For unknown to Jim, switchboard always check out with any enquiry such as Jim's with the relevant division, be it personnel, pathology, psychology or the social work sector, whatever. Most certainly, Dave Harrison, Senior Social Worker, was anything but Jim Holland's stereotypical image of a social soft sweetness of philanthropy. In fact, Dave Harrison was not soft inside but had solid steel for his guts and a mind of impregnable iron. But having said that, there was a highly unexpected twist, due to Dave Harrison's unpredictable line of thought, particularly in recent Rosedale months. For Dave had witnessed wind-ups, balls-ups, be they in clinical or security areas, and never had he ever been consulted for his opinions about such problems by top Rosedale management. In fact, it was far worse for Dave than simply that: he'd actually received the brunt of the blame for such problems – be they escapes of patients or what had been felt by some figures 'up top' to be excessive, unjustifiable expenditure upon rehabilitation schemes undertaken by the Social Work Department.

Dave was sick to death of it – what he so nauseatingly saw as totally misdirected flak upon himself and colleagues in what he knew was a grossly under-funded department of Rosedale. Not only under-funded, but totally misjudged by remote functionaries of management who always allocated the blame for their own failings of Rosedale mismanagement upon the easiest target, the one which found it hardest to defend itself – social work.

He had sadly witnessed an involuntary exodus of clinical care approaches whilst privatisational policies had simultaneously opened the Rosedale floodgates to a pathetic plethora of ambitious but irrelevant managers. So embittered had Dave Harrison become, that he was willing now to let guys such as Jim Holland actually damage Rosedale through adverse publications. Dave openly and gladly welcomed articles about inefficiency, red tape and a gravy train of parasitic administration.

Hence Dave's dilemma: to collude with Holland but not to arouse the suspicion of any other Rosedale personnel at all. So clearly, a rendezvous between Dave and Jim would have to be outside the Rosedale site, most certainly not within, for that would spell disaster.

And hence the actual bones of Dave's plan to deliberately leak classified data started to come together. Obviously it would be best if management fiddles such as the disappearances of cash in Rosedale – the one and a half million, for example – were highlighted, or the lavish managerial five-course lunches whilst patients had to just put up with sandwiches; but that was, Dave considered, both a bit risky and not quite dramatic enough for a paper like the *Mercury*. But what was good *Mercury* material was a story revolving around crime, especially insanity and crime; for the public would really lap that up.

And for a full day now Dave Harrison, unknown to all colleagues, had had his thinking cap firmly on, and a story suddenly emerged like a glorious gem. A gem of a particularly potent torpedo of adverse publicity, one which could quite violently rock a place which Dave Harrison no longer considered to be a hospital. A place which was for him no longer pleasant or worthwhile to work in, and most crucially of a highly dubious beneficence to its patients.

Most certainly it would be a surprise for Holland, a reporter expecting material about financial malpractice or bureaucratic bungling, when in actual fact it was to be much more exciting material; the kind so nicely congruent with recent public furore concerning what public and their MPs alike saw as extremely worrying, even menacing. It was about patients who possessed often quite serious criminal records coupled with mental disorders being allowed out of Rosedale on outings - be they shopping trips or visits home. Dave Harrison could so easily add fuel to such a fire of public uproar by giving information of a quite detailed, authentic nature for a paper to sensationalise to the hilt; it could maybe bust Rosedale wide open. This was Harrison's torpedo.

Harrison reached for the phone to make two calls - both in his calm, professional tone. He informed the switchboard that there was already an over-abundance of potential social workers, a surfeit in fact, and lied that he was acting upon instructions from the top that no more could be, or should be, taken on or even interviewed at present. Such a commanding dominance quelled any possible switchboard suspicion and could only melt their curiosity into an acquiescence of total acceptance. The other call, a brief one, was to the *Mercury* sub-office, to Jim Holland, the message from Dave brief and uncompromisingly direct. It was more like a format, a set of instructions of a procedure – one which Holland could only listen to and obey, for he had only the option of a non-story otherwise. The venue for the 'interview' was fixed – quite a nice cosy pub Dave added pleasantly – and his final telephone chuckle that Jim need not wear social worker attire of corduroys or suede shoes, simply dress as a press reporter instead.

Chapter Three

Rosedale had lots of different wards to accommodate what medical teams felt to be most receptive to needs of different patients. One in particular, often euphemistically termed the 'refractory ward' by hospital officialdom, was often a focus of attention. For patients called it not the refractory ward, but instead the punishment block – a ward they were sent to if they did anything wrong. 'Wrong' could encompass aggression to either staff or other patients, attempts to escape, or wanton damage of hospital property, even sometimes just being seen to be difficult to manage, unco-operative. Rosedale patient folklore had sinister tales of the beating up of patients sent to the block, or long periods spent in solitary confinement or drug over-sedations.

At seven a.m. this set of speculations was to be given the true test, the real 'McCoy' of an actual happening as the alarm bell to alert staff to a ward disturbance was activated, the ringing piercing all ears. A disturbance on Openview Ward in which an apparently much disturbed male patient in his mid-twenties had, it was said – quite unprovoked and for no apparent reason at all – become hostile and violent to a nurse whilst his shaving was being supervised just before breakfast. Staff, upon hearing the alarm had rushed from all directions to assist what they believed was an emergency situation of a fellow colleague being assaulted. Within less than thirty seconds there were numerous members of staff upon the actual scene of the incident. The patient was well pinned down to the bathroom floor, several staff tightly preventing him struggling, whilst a nurse was already loading up a syringe with a sedative drug in the adjacent ward clinic. As the injection was given the patient seemed to cease struggling, having given up the fight, the sting out of him gone, a coolness of mind apparent.

At the same time as the nurse in charge was filling in an assault and accident form for his injured student nurse colleague, another nurse was talking over the phone to staff upon Ironcare Ward. The decision was being made concerning the future situation of the patient who it was widely agreed upon by staff required a transfer to that Ward.

'I've already got clearance from Doctor Drake; he fully supports the decision, also it's to be very soon. I assume you've a vacancy?'

'Lots of vacancies,' replied a sombre deep drawl of a voice used to handling situations like that just gone. The dull drone added, 'Presumably there would be a stepping up of medication too?'

'Absolutely,' came the reply. 'Doctor Drake feels that a large increase is standard procedure and also perhaps something else too.'

'What's "something else" exactly?' said the drawl with a slightly raised tone betraying some curiosity.

'Don't know, but you'll find out when you see Drake – that should be in about ten minutes from now.'

'Oh, he's coming down personally to Ironcare is he? That's unusual; usually does it by way of the phone only.'

'Well, in this case he feels he needs to be involved, like I said – he may want to do something else other than just an upping of pills.'

'Right. By the way, was it bad?'

'What? The assault? No, just a cut lip, but that's not the point, is it?'

'No, any assault is heinous, that's why I work on Ironcare, and that's why Ironcare exists – for bad bastards like the one I'm taking off your ward – our new arrival in approximately what, ten minutes, did you say?'

'Less than. We'll get him shifted to you now. Happy hunting!'

Clearly Roberts had to be carried as he was well-nigh drugged to insensibility, down the stairs and along a dingy maze of medical smelling corridors. Such a mix of medical odours colluded with the smell from the main kitchens of a pungent stew, giving a typical sickly hospital nasal cocktail.

Doctor Drake was waiting, his eyes grey and grim, his mouth a thin angry line.

'Into the ward clinic,' he snapped, as four staff carrying patient Roberts followed Drake's quite deliberate march towards the clinic. The clinic was a treatment room which was badly ventilated and always had a stale smell; it had bandages, plasters, resuscitation equipment and also some mysterious apparatus which was not often used. But it was Doctor Drake's intention to use it now.

'ECT,' he barked, pointing to the electric shock gear contained in a small black box in a corner.

'Obviously with anaesthetic and a muscle relaxant?' said the charge nurse expecting an automatic reply of 'yes'.

'No,' said Drake. 'No anaesthetic, no muscle relaxant either.'

All of the six nurses present in the clinic looked up askance, for they knew what Drake's decision, the actual practical implications, meant for Roberts. It most surely meant a procedure now largely illegal in most psychiatric units in the modern world. It meant invariably excruciating pain for a patient who unfortunately had to have it: 'raw' electric shock therapy. But there were other reasons which caused the nurses present to feel concern too. First of all, ECT, Electro-Convulsive Therapy, the method of passing an electric current through a patient's brain, is usually a 'treatment' applied to states of acute depression. Those nursing staff all were aware of that fact, particularly that Roberts was anything but depressed, merely a schizophrenic who had shown signs of aggressiveness. Usually a suitable treatment outcome would be merely to give extra chemotherapy, that is, drugs administered either orally, by injection, or both. This had already occurred and, judging by Roberts unperturbed, semi-sleeping face, would warrant no more clinical intervention. Certainly all six experienced well-qualified nurses present felt this to be the case. But not so for Doctor Clifford Drake. He felt different about it. The fact he was a consultant also meant that he effectively held the reins. If he felt, as he quite categorically did, that electric shocks should be given, then electric shocks it was to be.

Reluctantly the nurses strapped Roberts very firmly onto the clinic bed so his limbs were bound fast. Often if not strapped securely, raw ECT could, due to its shock sensation, result in dislocated limbs, even broken bones due to an over-reaction of a subject's nervous system. Also a rubber device was pushed between Robert's teeth to prevent him perhaps biting off his tongue – again a possibility when electrically shocked. Drake watched the preparations unmoved, almost, it appeared, impatiently, strongly desiring to activate the machine.

'Are we ready?' he said, and without waiting for an answer pressed the switch. With no attempt at exaggeration, it could be truly said that, despite six strong pairs of arms, Roberts still was agonizingly able to suddenly bear a grimace of great pain and arch his body a good eighteen inches up and clear off the bed. Such was the pain and Robert's bodily resistance to the electrically-induced convulsion that the sudden shock of seizure and reaction to white hot electrical burning sensation caused cerebral agony. After a few moments it was over, Roberts limp on the bed, unconscious.

'He'll come round quite soon I imagine,' said Drake. 'I think it should be fine, but if not, any side-effects of this let me know, okay?'

As for Roberts' expression, it was a thousand very recently abnormally etched lines by no other sculptor than sadistically induced electric pain. Again, without any exaggeration, Roberts and others of similar misfortune were lucky to literally still be alive. Yet, in a way, it was worse than death, for such ECT sessions could quite well be repeated for Roberts or any other patients by the Doctor Drakes of this world. The agony could occur, could be dished out again so easily. And again and again after that, whilst held compulsorily in Rosedale. There was nothing the patients of Rosedale could do about it either. It was a living death.

Bob Driscoll was sipping a steaming mug of coffee at his mid-morning break when the phone rang. Charge Nurse Humphries said that he had tried to contact Doctor Drake about patient Roberts who seemed to be suffering worrying side-effects, but couldn't locate Drake anywhere. Bob Driscoll, with a touch of concern in his voice, assured Humphries that he'd stand in for Drake as regards Roberts and be along straightaway. Certainly for Bob that wasn't easy – he was snowed under with work – reports to compile on patients on prison sections being temporarily held in Rosedale for medical reports, conferences to attend, meetings and yet more meetings. Still, his morning happened by chance to be uncluttered, unusually free.

Doctor Driscoll was horrified. Roberts' open, sagging mouth looked as if he'd got both jaws broken as saliva abundantly drooled forth. His eyes seemed to be vacant, almost unseeing, his speech well-nigh unintelligible, just an incoherent virtually inaudible muttering.

'Fill me in on this Humphries, will you?' said Driscoll in a very serious tone, 'and don't have cold feet about Doctor Drake's reaction to what you feel.'

'That's the problem. In a nutshell, Doctor Driscoll, I can't break ethicality by criticism of a consultant,' said a somewhat worried Humphries.

'Even though you feel you should and would very much like to? Yes?'

'Yes,' said Humphries in a quiet voice, his difficult dilemma betrayed by his timorous reply.

'Well, Drake's not here, but I am, and as a senior consultant I'm in charge, so spit it out. Do you feel Drake's mishandled this one or not?'

Humphries paused at a verbal crossroads of a suitable reply. Then he took a deep breath and spoke. 'Well, not in a particularly diagnostic capacity, no.'

Driscoll lost his cool and angrily met Humphries' evasive, indecisive eyes. 'Well then, in exactly what bloody capacity? Treatment, procedure, accountability or what? Do you quite simply mean that Drake "ballsed-it" all up. For God's sake, speak man! Commit yourself!'

'Yes,' said a still faltering Humphries, 'I think possibly ECT was okay, but in no way should it have been administered as it actually was upon Roberts.'

'*Actually was?*' questioned an intrigued Driscoll. 'Tell me how it was given. There's something you're not telling me, eh?'

Humphries spat it out. 'It was given straight, Doctor.'

'Straight? You mean raw? No anaesthetic or muscle relaxant injections beforehand?'

'That's it Doctor, absolutely so; I did remark upon it to Doctor Drake briefly afterwards, though.'

'But to no avail?'

'To no avail.'

'He just more or less reminded you of your position and his authority, yes?'

'Yes sir, that's the score.'

Doctor Driscoll blew out his cheeks in annoyed exasperation. 'Good grief! We're still in the medical middle-ages!' He pointed to Roberts' shaking body. 'Look at him; he's bloody fortunate to have not died! In future when something like this blows up, inform me, okay? Not Drake. Is that crystal clear to you and your entire day-shift staff? The poor bastard's lucky to be still alive.' He paused, his anger slowly relenting as he forced himself to get it all into a rough perspective. He spoke quietly in a rather resigned, almost fatalistic way. 'Still, I suppose this issue is nothing new in a place like this, and it's no surprise that it was handled by Drake in his invariably mistaken way.'

Doctor Driscoll stood up, cast a sympathetic glance across the dormitory to where Roberts was sitting, still shaking in his electrically created tremors, and told Humphries to give pain-killers for Robert's headaches and a fortnight's rest, away from occupational activities in the patients' workshop. He met Humphries' eyes. 'Remember, call me in future if you need a doctor on this ward. Call me, not some incompetent ignoramus, is that clear?'

Humphries gave a nod, and Driscoll marched out of the ward, but not back to his office, but to another ward, Danny Broughton's ward . . .

He walked past a handful of patients cleaning out the ward kitchen and a nurse showing round a couple of curious visitors, explaining how a typical Rosedale Ward was run – day-time routines, patients' activities, staff supervision of such activities, and various other psychiatric speel – and kept walking towards the far dormitory. Suddenly his purposeful march soothingly slowed down, his face becoming less rigid, more softened and a mellow composure of pleasure settled upon him.

Driscoll found it difficult to convince himself of Danny's essentially human essence, for how, he wondered, could a beautiful god be so irreducibly mortal, so mundanely human.

Daniel stirred, flexed his limbs into a stretch and spoke. 'You look angry, Bob. I've done nothing wrong have I? Please don't increase the Largactil, it makes me fat, makes me tired, makes me eat too much.'

Bob Driscoll seemed as if he'd been hit by a freak giant wave, so taken aback at what he rightly felt was Danny's verbal catalogue of unwarranted suspicion. 'No, no, no. I've just come to see if you'd like some fresh air. It's nice out in the grounds, maybe a cup of tea, a smoke, a joke, chat, whatever. Better than being cooped up in here.'

'I've no parole as yet,' said Daniel fatalistically. 'They keep punishing me, sometimes spy on me, always watching me.'

'Whose they?' said a bewildered Driscoll.

'The whole staff rarely leave me alone, at peace. They won't let me be.'

'Nonsense!' boomed Driscoll. 'Come on! Shoes on, coat on, we're going to blow the cobwebs away.'

'You'll let them know about me out on parole then? They might think I'm going over their heads to you, the consultant.'

'Don't worry about it,' Bob said quickly, pecking Daniel's very white cheeks which reddened somewhat immediately after the kissing and Bob sensed passion, or perhaps just a slight embarrassment. Bob couldn't tell which and didn't ask. They left the musty surgically smelling stuffiness of the ward and within minutes found themselves amongst large cedar trees, greenhouses and disused stone fountains.

The spacious, pretty, century-old Rosedale grounds were lovely to walk around or sit down in, either in summer or in winter. Even winter had a nice crisp frostiness, icicles growing down from old iron guttering. The mellow red brick and tons of slates upon roofs had easily defied all weathers and erosive attacks for over a hundred years. And that long century had an amazing silence to it, a secrecy of which so few people of the outside world ever really knew. At one time patients who died whilst actually in Rosedale, that is the long termers seen to be chronically ill and unsuitable for release, were often buried at some place within the actual grounds. At that very moment

Danny was thinking along very similar lines.

'We might be actually standing above a dead patient this very moment,' Daniel hesitatingly said. 'Walking on an asylum inmate's grave!'

'Maybe,' said Bob, a little disconcerted at Danny's sudden flicker of morbidity. 'But we are still alive and kicking, are we not?' he said pleasantly, trying to inject an air of optimism.

'Some of us only just,' Danny replied. 'In fact I may myself be dead already, nothing inside me, just darkness.' He paused then continued his melancholy murmuring. 'You are my only saviour, doctor, my only light in the world, and yet you do not look like Jesus at all.'

'How should, or does, Jesus look then Danny?' Bob said, pressing his curious angle of enquiry into what seemed a depressing moratorium, a moribund confused recantation he'd hoped he might today have avoided.

But there was no respite, all to no avail as Danny, head down, became misty eyed, saying he regretted his existence of purgatory.

'I cannot ever see life as a privilege, only a curse,' he desperately said. 'You're lucky in not being a member of us.'

'A member? Of what?' asked Driscoll perplexed.

'Of all those, who without conscious choice had it all taken away from them, on admission to places such as this.'

'What taken away?'

'The right to a normal, happy life. Instead only black nights, black days, black food, black thoughts, black pictures, poems, paper, pens, records, lighters, pocket money, cigarettes – every bloody black thing,' he said, almost shouting, then starting to shake. It seemed he had started to cry. Bob Driscoll's face was a classic portrait of helpless marooned sympathy and understanding, but deep unhappiness. Anybody could be vulnerable to the kind of breakdown which his precious, still-shaking totem of love had once, so tragically and undeservedly succumbed.

It was getting a bit cold, and a rather uncomfortable late

November breeze was creeping around them. 'A mug of tea then?' suggested Driscoll, as he pulled up his collar and squeezed Daniel's cold white hand.

The canteen was noisy, as it usually was, with hot, stale air and very thick smoke. Driscoll offered Daniel a cigarette, they sipped their drinks and their eyes surveyed the other patients.

'Most of these have got parole,' Daniel said, 'but nobody likes me to have parole because they think I'm too dangerous.'

'Oh! come off it,' Driscoll replied. 'You wouldn't hurt a fly. There's no violence in you, never has been. I'll personally see to it that you'll get plenty of parole, to get you out and about, ready for the really big one – out of Rosedale.'

'You think so? Really?'

'Yes,' said an exasperated Driscoll, 'really. You could be out of this place in six months. It's a piece of cake, a doddle, there are far worse cases in here than you. You're all right Danny. Smashing to be with, and if it could be one day, to enjoyably live with!'

'You're a married, respectable man!' Daniel exclaimed.

'So bloody what! If I choose you and still stay with Gill it's no big sweat. In fact if I so wish, I can keep as many relationships going as I can possibly manage. Like I say, Danny, it's no big sweat.'

'No big sweat at all?' said Daniel in deep rumination.

'Don't worry your head about my problems. In fact they're not even problems at all, all part of being a consultant with obligations to others.'

Daniel smiled. 'The helping, caring profession. Yes?'

Driscoll laughed. 'Yes, that's it, that's what it's all about, what I was born for, to be the softest, kindest creature on earth!' They both laughed, blowing out smoke and lighting one cigarette after another.

Suddenly a device attached to Doctor Driscoll's belt gave a repeated bleep indicating he was required on a ward.

'We'll have to make tracks. I'm needed, Danny,' he said, kissing him when outside the canteen. 'I'll let you back onto your ward.'

'It's been nice,' Daniel said. 'You've cheered me up a bit.'

'Good,' said Driscoll, passing Daniel a half-full pack of cigarettes. 'Have these,' he said, and added, 'All right for money?'

'Not too bad,' Daniel said, and at that, Driscoll also passed him a couple of fivers and some loose change.

'See you soon,' said Bob, as they departed at Daniel's ward, and Daniel again said thanks for what he felt had been a good man to talk to, so much so that at that actual moment, Danny Broughton didn't feel quite so lonely any more.

With Danny still very much in his thoughts, Doctor Driscoll nonetheless still managed to act with a cool, objective, professional demeanour. Within minutes of leaving Danny he was sitting on the side of a middle-aged patient's bed.

'And there's nothing left to live for now people know or say I'm mad,' the unhappy, hunched up figure, sadly said.

'There's everything to live for, work for, try for, love for. Don't you see,' said Doctor Driscoll, 'that your life is your most precious unique gift.

'But where now is the meaning to it all? I'm on the scrap heap of a society which can only laugh at me now, point fun at a loony like me.'

'You're no loony, but I'm going to let the staff give you tablets; not many, just for the time being. Okay?'

'Not ECT for God's sake? Don't give me that, please, no shocks!'

'For goodness sake no,' said Driscoll. 'Just some very mild anti-depressants, just for a very short time, okay?'

Doctor Driscoll had a word with the nurse in charge, a pretty brunette, with hair piled up into a bun. He asked her her name.

'Kim Hesketh,' she replied warmly. 'How often, the prothiadine tablets you've prescribed?'

'Just at breakfast and bedtime and I'll be along in a few days to review it, see how he's doing. There doesn't seem much cause for concern.' They parted company on a dingy, rather drab corridor, Doctor Driscoll saying he needed some lunch.

Driscoll had done no more than light a much-needed cigarette when he looked up to see a rapidly walking figure coming his way: Doctor Drake. Driscoll decided to speak, although it was difficult to be polite and pleasant.

'A damned busy morning, that's for sure.'

'Isn't it just,' replied Drake, also attempting to avoid a strain, even a potential *contretemps*.'

But Bob Driscoll, no matter how he tried, could not avoid his temptation to add just a tiny bit of criticism, disagreement about Drake's handling of Roberts earlier on.

'A little bit extreme maybe?' he said.

'What?' said Drake defensively, knowing exactly what Driscoll was referring to.

Driscoll sensed this deliberate ignorance.

'I'm referring to what you're alluding to: Roberts, the ECT, all that sort of stuff.'

'I don't wish to discuss it, quite frankly . . .'

'Well, I'm pretty sure that Roberts would like a say in it, which he can't due to what seems like possible permanent brain damage or severe memory loss, to say the least . . .'

'I've told you once and that's quite sufficient. I am not willing to discuss how I individually practice my job. There's nothing to discuss.'

'Well, maybe not right now, but there could well be a lot to discuss in the not too distant future, if there are atrocious repeats of this morning. Can't you take a subtle hint? Lay off with the philistinism, it's not the middle ages.'

Drake shook his head sideways indicating his agreement to disagree, and said it might be useful if such statements of Driscoll were revealed to Ralph Johnson, the Rosedale Medical

Director, under a heading of totally needless and meddlesome unprofessionalism. 'For,' said Drake. 'professional backbiting is unhealthy, the patients suffer as a result.'

Drake walked past an angrily stupefied Bob Driscoll, who could only reel at Drake's just-stated hypocritical contradiction. Behaviour earlier in the morning so incompatibly juxtaposed alongside a statement just spoken about professional camaraderie and consequent implications for patient welfare.

'Most truly,' Driscoll uttered to himself, 'that person to whom I've just spoken is unequivocally and dangerously mad.'

Chapter Four

'And I suppose that's hospital policy too?' said Luke Lloyd Evans, stifling a bored yawn.

'No, not *just* hospital policy at all,' countered a rather niggly Ralph Johnson, the Rosedale number one, the medical director. 'It's my policy too! Always has been so, and as far as I'm concerned whilst I remain in this post, it always will be.'

'Cold feet of timorousness, or just an accumulated conservatism?' prodded Luke provocatively.

Ralph Johnson was seen to momentarily bite, a flash of impatience crossing his usually ultra diplomatic cool demeanour. He reacted to Luke's comment on an equally personal level. 'The sort of airy-fairy comment I'd expect from a psychologist, a typical adventurous, but unrealistic view adopted by one in a position with very little face to lose. A typical psychologist's type of question.'

This time, even top grade clinical psychologist Luke Lloyd Evans had cause to bite, to react at what he perceived as an uncalled for remark.

'And just what is a "typical" psychologist?' he said in a tone betraying a glimmer of resentment, even professionally wounded indignation. Ralph Johnson beamed and rubbed together his bony hands. 'Oh! I'm so glad you asked me that one, Luke. I've a wonderful definition, and I've been waiting absolutely ages for the opportunity – the ideal moment – to proudly tell you!'

'What?' said Luke, expecting some kind of convoluted slight.

'A psychologist,' said Ralph, 'is not simply an ostrich blind to total circumstantial factors with its unheeding, unreasonable head in the sand, but also a person suffering from a serious condition of an unaquaintance with reality.'

'I see,' said Luke thoughtfully. 'I take it that I'm a deprived, totally theoretical child, one in nappies who shouldn't ever be allowed to enter the vicious streets of an adult world?' He continued. 'A person whose only useful home is an academic establishment of millions of textbooks but very few people. Yes?'

Aware of Luke's heavy, syrupy sarcasm, Ralph Johnson realised he'd actually, perhaps for the very first time, managed to get under Luke's ultra-cool skin. Ralph sat back in his soft leather armchair behind a desk littered with dirty coffee cups and spilt sugar.

'Okay,' he said, 'enough of jokes, mutual recriminations, professionalised back-biting, grudges, whatever. Let's try and prevent a complete exodus of any notions of teamwork that preciously remain, shall we?'

Luke, equally sensitive, nodded his agreement, a character rarely prone to enjoy feuds.

'We don't want word games, we need to sort out this great pile of crap on our doorstep. If not, Ralph, I agree: Rosedale may soon no longer be our home, there will be no doorsteps for either of us, *any* of us for that matter.'

'Good!' said Ralph Johnson. 'Realism in the situation. It was my perceived lack of it in you that caused me to be maybe a bit critical, so no more of the time-wasting, picking holes, at least not for this present pit of headaches, okay?'

'Okay, and, yes, I fully see it's one hell of a headache,' said a serious Luke Lloyd Evans. 'The public really hate our guts, yes?'

'Perhaps they hate us even more than that,' said Ralph sadly. 'Almost a crusade to cripple us.'

'And in so doing,' added Luke, 'do what they have for over

a century dreamed of doing; to crucify Rosedale.'

'In a nutshell, I couldn't agree more, Luke,' said Ralph, rubbing his bloodshot eyes. 'I just couldn't agree more.'

'So where do we proceed?' Luke said, always optimistic, if occasionally unrealistic.

'By tightening up,' said Ralph.

'Upon exactly what area? Security? Rehabilitation trips? Patient privileges? Rights? Visiting hours? Visitors themselves? What?' Luke said most truly bereft of Ralph's intentions.

Ralph Johnson stared around the room. It was perhaps a full minute before he very carefully gave an answer.

'As a general rule of thumb – virtually all Rosedale therapeutic services. A well-organised, recognised, co-ordinated endeavour to make the uneasy tension between the need for security and the need for rehabilitation smoother. It can be done too.'

'Yes, maybe it can,' said Luke genuinely and constructively, 'because it's only a very small number of patients who escape and get highlighted by the media. Most patients are no problem at all.'

'Correct,' said Ralph. 'All that's required is a more substantive assessment procedure by us, a more rigorous rehabilitation programme of patient evaluation.'

'So if we get more stringent in our "rehab" selection procedures, we don't have to necessarily sacrifice any accompanying amount of actual patient "rehab" outings.'

'Exactly, just as many patients out in the community on shopping excursions as ever before, but the "thoroughly assessed to our satisfaction" right type of patient.'

'Somebody who doesn't "balls" it all up and ruin it for the rest, yes?'

'Yes, ones who don't run off in town away from their nurse escorts with crazy ideas to escape. In this way we'll survive the press in future, and our open public disclosure of this new policy now should help us ride any immediate stick we're getting, as in fact we are at present.'

'So a low profile image on patients' outside trips, and a more rigorous selection procedure of patients for such possible "rehab" schemes, to be undertaken by all respective medical teams.'

Ralph's face relaxed, his features, posture at ease. 'You've got it in one Luke. Sorry about earlier – I maybe misjudged you . . .'

Ralph phoned for fresh coffee and Suzy White brought in the tray of cups and jugs with a lovely chinking sound. Suzy, the Rosedale number two, who already had reached dizzy heights of Deputy Medical Director, remained in Ralph's spacious, if rather musty suite, tinkering about with a word-processor.

Suddenly the phone rang and any voice on it, or spoken into it, could be heard by all present in the room owing to an attached amplification device. Suzy was listening as Ralph was talking, whereas Luke was absentmindedly musing to himself over future logistics of patient rehabilitation programmes in which he would be involved concerning relevant psychological input.

Ralph seemed a little confused and concerned as he listened to a caller who gave his name as Mr Frank Farley. Suzy's shrewd ears pricked up; she'd heard that name before. Ralph seemed not to be getting much chance to speak, ask any questions himself. Instead a slightly excitable Frank Farley was asking all sorts of questions in what seemed a rather pushy voice.

Ralph at last managed to get a word in. 'It all seems somewhat undercover, almost manipulative, Mr Farley. We are by no means obliged to give you that information or any at all, even to speak to you or any *Mercury* staff . . .'

'Let's quit formalities. Call me Frank. Is there somebody else perhaps? Less busy, more forthcoming? Public relations perhaps?'

Ralph paused, weighing up the pros and cons of a potentially difficult situation. If he simply slammed the phone down then this Mr Farley would be even more inquisitive, more tenacious, maybe snubbed, and ruthless to Rosedale. Ralph had to seem unruffled, play it cool. Suzy White was just about to ask Ralph if he'd let her onto the phone to apply a softening, unserious woman's diplomatic touch when Ralph said to Frank he was putting him through on a direct extension line to Personnel.

Ralph put down the phone. 'Trish Turner's handling it,' he confidently said.

'Our trouble-shooter *par excellence*?' Luke asked.

'Yes, she's good at this sort of thing,' Ralph exclaimed, sipping his black coffee.

'And I'm not?' muttered a rather annoyed Suzy White, pretending to be busy with a pile of floppy disks and other processor paraphernalia. Ralph heard her undertones of resentment, feeling a little bit ashamed that perhaps he may have made an error in having not delegated Suzy after all. Luke cleverly tried to defuse the strained atmosphere by way of a mild, lightening comment.

'There's little need it seems for an amplified phone it would appear,' as he reached to a close-by circuitry device and effectively switched off amplification.

'Now at least nobody present will be aware, and . . .'

Ralph cut in forcefully. 'Now look Luke, we don't need fuel on a fire. Perhaps I get a little tactless at times, for that I apologise – sorry, Suzy, I guess I was confused by the caller and questions he fired at me.'

'Oh it's all right,' lied Suzy with a false smile, unsatisfied by Ralph's apology.

Ralph Johnson got to his feet and sauntered across the wide, rather untidy room. Strewn about were many volumes of outdated books, many unread by himself, all gathering dust, and lots of unexciting, equally dusty pictures on the walls. The large room certainly needed redecorating, a lot of shabby furniture thrown out; the generally ancient layout mirroring much of Rosedale's decaying face of lagging behind the times.

'Don't you see,' said Luke, 'that we're letting all this recent press business get to us.'

'Yes,' said Ralph, 'it's not for us to suffer. It should be the Frank Farleys of this God-forsaken age.'

'An age, incidentally,' added an abstract Luke, 'of what has been recently described as "individualistic attrition!"'

'What's he on about?' said Suzy to Ralph.

'I'm as flummoxed as you, Suzy,' said Ralph. 'In normal discourse for us novices please, Luke.'

'We're all desperate today – clutching at straws, divided, atomised – but that's no solution, it compounds the problem even more.'

'You've totally lost me,' Suzy said.

Luke's hands waved to illustrate his point to be understandably put across. 'We need a collective, united front, human cohesion in a growing inhuman age . : .'

The three gulped down what had by now become only lukewarm coffee, and then the phone rang again. Ralph grabbed the receiver listening intently, shocked at the same time to find that Luke had become a little mischievous – Luke had surreptitiously managed to switch on the amplified phone device again.

Suzy spoke. 'A practical joker and psychologist in the same surprise package – what a lucky bag we've got with us today!'

Ralph didn't hear Suzy's quip, being too engrossed in Trish Turner's rather garbled message. Suzy, as she listened, couldn't help but become more and more victorious, the gloat of triumph spreading through her widening mouth, eyes beginning to gleam. Trish Turner was telling Ralph that all the previous hours' conversational confusion and disarray might well have been avoided had Ralph let Suzy White initially handle the whole Farley business. Trish was at pains to say that she, herself, felt rather ill-equipped to deal with Frank Farley's clever, manipulative edge of questioning.

'I simply couldn't put the phone down on him, Ralph,' said

Trish.

'Why ever not?' said a rather demanding Ralph.

'He made it clear that the *Mercury* are very much wised-up on all recent Rosedale events, which could so easily be dynamite if exploited by a popular tabloid . . .'

'What does he know exactly? Is it about admin, pathology, ward activities, patient outings, management, or what?'

'I can't say, Ralph,' Trish stressed rather timidly, 'due to my finding it difficult to actually deal with such an unfamiliar kind of call . . .'

'But you're our best, Trish; you've never dropped a clanger, and surely this Farley guy is only a small fish from a rather undistinguished paper anyway.'

'No, you couldn't be more wrong, Ralph. He's good, and quite a senior reporter, and the *Mercury* has a fairly widespread readership, the circulation always rising, particularly due to stories like the one Farley wishes to hatch now.'

Ralph blew out his cheeks. 'So what do you suppose we do, or I do?'

Trish paused, took a deep breath and spoke as her true convictions dictated, the smile still growing more and more radiant upon Suzy White. 'I suggest you don't so often choose me in such difficult press matters any longer, Ralph, at least not of this actual nature.'

'And so you're saying what exactly, Trish?'

'That Suzy White would be more competent at this kind of sensitive issue than me.'

Chapter Five

'Obviously quite a genuine attempt,' said the senior nurse twiddling with some coins in his pocket.

'Obviously,' said a serious-as-ever Doctor Drake.

'And one,' continued the nurse, 'most certainly not motivated by attention seeking.'

'Absolutely. The entire fabric of the incident speaks for itself,' commented a furrowed, frowning Drake.

Both of them stared silently upwards at the chain of dressing-gown cords knotted still firmly to the steel curtain rail.

'I know exactly what you're thinking,' said Drake. 'The kind of question you want to ask, and to ask myself in particular . . .'

'What, doctor?' asked the nurse, a little bowled over with Drake's grandiose medical ego, and also, it seemed, the self-proclaimed status of a mind reader.

'You want to know what the appropriate prescribed treatment is in this situation, but as I am the one to make such a decision, what treatment I personally think is suitable, yes?'

'Yes,' said the nurse, already thinking that if not just arrogant, Drake was also decidedly odd as a person to talk to. Doctor Drake seemed extremely difficult to describe, a sort of emotional hollowness, a personality without warm substance, conversing with him being not dissimilar to talking into a machine. Such a discovery by anyone who spoke to him triggered a realisation of frightful fear when it was borne in mind his actual job - his awesome power over the quality of life, future prospects, hopes to be either gladly realised or dashed to damnation – seemed to possess the power, almost, of life and death. But it was even deeper, grimmer than that. For not only could a powerless patient be painfully electrically shocked as a result of a decision by Drake, but there was no accountability required of Drake as to the pros and cons of such a decision; he was immune from criticism. The professionalism of a senior consultant's post rendered all opposition futile due to his ostensibly medically specialised knowledge. Nobody below him in the entire hospital could reproach him, no matter how strong their grievance, due to his position which rested quite legitimately on his monopoly of medical knowledge.

Right now the nurse was waiting, as well as anticipating, Drake's opinions on the incident of an attempted suicide. In a way the nurse felt a bit irritated because he knew, whatever his own personal views were about this current issue and, even if allowed to state them, Doctor Drake wouldn't take any notice anyway. Yes, Drake would listen to views of nursing staff but effectively such opinions, no matter how clinically sound or reasonable, would cut no ice in what action was to be taken, and Drake knew that very well indeed.

'Well then,' said Drake, about to answer what was his own actual question, 'it would appear that the last six months of chemotherapy in the form of anti-depressant tablets don't seem to have fulfilled their purpose.'

'Agreed,' said the increasingly apprehensive nurse.

'And,' Drake continued, 'ECT has already been tried and failed with him before, yes?'

'Yes,' said the nurse, having to keep agreeing with Drake, although he much desired to disagree. It was useless to say more about the patient concerned, knowing that Drake was only utilizing him as a kind of pathetic wireless to legitimate and to reinforce the decision he was soon to make, and had in fact already arrived at. Charge Nurse Robinson knew what it would most certainly be, the decision of the actual 'treatment' Drake would prescribe, and Robinson was dead set against such a ruthless course of action, especially having to be unavoidably present with Drake as such a terrible prescription was being formulated. Robinson felt he was being used, used by an obnoxious doctor to quite powerlessly collude with, be a party to, a shared, mutually-arrived at, agreed-upon decision. He was right and yet there was absolutely nothing he could do about it. His predicament was particularly painful because very soon his own colleagues, fellow nurses, would reproach him in their mistaken belief that he had quite willingly supported Drake.

'And part of the problem,' added Drake, 'is of course the essentially temporary, and hence limited, effectiveness of treatments for him so far prescribed.'

Robinson cut in as boldly as he felt his subordinate position allowed him to. 'But there are quite a wide range of anti-depressant drugs, many of which we haven't yet tried upon him . . .'

'No, I think we have tried enough already, all to no therapeutic avail. We've exhausted our chemical arsenal. I'm afraid something else, something more long lasting is required. You see, we cannot uselessly keep duplicating all previously failed treatments, we need to attain a state of biological permanence.'

'Neurological intervention, you mean?' asked Robinson. 'Psycho-surgical measures?'

'I'm afraid so,' said a deadly serious Drake. 'But of course a second medical opinion shall be sought.'

Robinson was rapidly getting the picture of all of Drake's machinations – and didn't like it at all. For the desire of Drake to ask for a second opinion, another consultant's views upon the appropriate treatment, was merely for Drake to cover himself, his own safety net in getting his decision shared so that if there were any recriminations, subsequent to the brain surgery, then Drake would not, and could not, be held solely, individually responsible. That situation was how it always worked out – to Drake's benefit. It worked because a calling of a second opinion was a mere formality – the second opinion was virtually always in agreement and supported the first. This was due to a doctor such as Drake being himself the person to have the prerogative of choosing the actual consultant who was to give a second opinion, the psychiatric assessment of a patient's required type of medical intervention. Also, these two views invariably were mutually reinforcing, very seldom in dispute. Drake knew all of this inside out, as for that matter did Charge Nurse Robinson, who strongly felt that as usual, Doctor Drake went to often badly thought out, callous extremes. Doctor Drake lit his little pipe, looked at his watch and spoke. 'Well, I suppose we might as well go to the sick bay and see him, yes?'

Robinson was inwardly fuming as he pondered upon Drake's utter iciness – as if Drake felt it a mere token, a superficial formality to see the actual patient concerned before authorising such a major and life-long damaging method of treatment which was to very soon be dished out – whether the patient desired it or not. Robinson and Drake walked into the ward office, and Drake picked up the phone saying to Robinson that he was trying to locate another doctor on site to be the one to give a second opinion.

A couple of minutes passed and Drake replaced the receiver smiling confidently. 'A Doctor Peterson will be available soon after we've reached our own views.'

Upon arrival in the hospital sick bay a nurse was attempting to comfort and console what seemed an extremely distraught, anxious young man. From time to time he could be seen to place his head in his hands and burst into tears. Doctor Drake advanced towards the bed. 'Okay,' he said quite brusquely to the nurse. 'I'll take over now.'

'Would you like me to remain though, Doctor?' the nurse said. 'He's extremely upset . . .'

'No, I'll handle this,' said Drake. 'He's probably more confused than anything else.'

'But,' said the nurse, 'unhappy also . . .'

'I'll be the judge of that!' snapped Drake, waving his hand at him to signify that he should go through the exit door so as to leave him alone. 'And,' said Drake to Robinson, 'I think you could use a coffee. I'll be quite all right left alone with the patient.'

Again Robinson was reminded of his own insignificance in Doctor Drake's eyes. Just a superfluous dogsbody in a white coat who dished out patients' meals, medicines; no other duties seemingly allowed to competently perform. After many years of psychiatric nursing, Robinson cursed himself for having ever had the life wasting stupidity to embark upon such a choice of career. He hated contemporary health policies of psychiatric hospital privatisation, his own powerlessness in the medical team of which he was supposed to play a key role, but most of all, he had a caustic distaste, a vitriolic hatred for Doctor Drake. If there was one most desired wish allocated to Robinson, it would be to see Drake humiliated into disgrace in front of all his colleagues, sacked, struck off the mental health register forever. As Robinson stepped out of the door to leave Drake and the patient alone, he desperately hoped that one day, one massively sweet, revengeful day, that Drake's demise would come. He lit a cigarette to try and help him calm down, by now badly needing both nicotine and caffeine.

'A bit of a silly thing to do, yes?' said Drake with an unsympathetic expression on his face.

'It was not so simple, so clear as you think,' said Steven.

'Not so simple? What then?' questioned Drake.

'My dad died nine months ago, and also a recent decision made said my parole applications were turned down . . .'

'Yes, but is that any excuse, any logical reason to try and hang yourself? Tell me, tell me now. Well?'

'I can't stand it here, I've no future . . .'

'You say no future?'

'None worth talking about, living for . . .'

'You'd feel better off out of it, happily removed, yes? Contentedly dead?'

'I don't know. It's too confusing, depressing.'

'You've just mentioned the key to unlock it all, your attitude and the suicidal caper of last night.'

'What?'

'Why, Steven! Depression of course. Can't you see it all now? Can't you understand? You are morbidly afflicted with an unhealthy melancholia, the state of which requires certain treatments.'

'Not ECT for pity's sake, I couldn't stand the pain . . .'

'No, just a little alteration of the way you think, how you feel, that's all . . .'

'Painless?'

'Absolutely. There will then be so much of a life worth living for, which at present you feel unable to see. Doctor Peterson and I have discussed such matters. It is entirely to help nobody but yourself . . .'

Steven was about to ask many questions, all of the utmost urgency, but Doctor Drake was already leaving, pushing ajar the exit door.

'Doctor Drake,' said Steven, frightened and in fear of what treatment was to be given. 'I'd like to have some idea of . . .'

But Drake did not hear Steven's desperate request, for the door had opened and closed; Doctor Drake had gone.

Like some sinister soccer stadium the glaring lights remorselessly flooded down. The operating theatre specializing in removal of cerebral tissue was Steven's last fully humanly perceived scene, whilst his brain remained physically intact. Untampered, still the same. But in approximately three quarters of an hour he would no longer be completely human, and with such a plight correspondingly possess only half a personality.

Straight away, half-masked faces of brain surgeons started the task at hand. Neurological modification intended to remove certain nerve tissues, or more precisely to widen, to split up, to divide nerve tracts or pathways. This procedure was to have the tenuous outcome of reducing an individual's capacity for extremes of behaviour – usually upon aggressive personalities, but also for depressives whose behavioural manifestations were fuelled by psychosis.

Such was Steven's fate. In many ways to have been found dead on the end of his self-made noose a couple of mornings before would have been infinitely more merciful than this state of affairs now being undergone. A cabbage of an irreversible state; no going back to, no return to a previous personality intactness, only forwards to plod through remaining years of a half-life. Such purgatory was growing inexorably closer as bloody swabs of cotton wool were dropped into a nearby plastic bin.

'And the reasons given?' muttered a partially preoccupied junior surgeon.

'Regenerative schizophrenia with unpredictable depressive predispositions,' replied the equally absorbed senior surgeon.

'Acute depression obviously, I assume?' continued the rather curious junior member.

To this, the senior surgeon paused momentarily to carefully consider an accurate reply to his colleague's question. 'Not absolutely certain about that – degree of acuteness; a rather woolly report and recommendations presented to us really . . .'

'Which consultant, might I ask? Perhaps I might know whoever . . .'

'Oh you will! Most certainly you'll be familiar with Doctor Drake, I'm sure! Does the name ring a bell?'

'Again?' said the rather astounded junior neurological member. 'Do you realise all cases we handle for standard frontal leucotomies are overwhelmingly those recommended by Doctor Drake?'

'I'm perfectly aware of that; still, I do suppose that in a roundabout way he knows his psychiatric stuff – he's qualified to the hilt. Did you know that?'

'No, I didn't,' said the young surgeon thoughtfully, 'but I know one thing . . .'

'Yes?'

'All leucotomies over the last twelve months in Rosedale have been mainly those recommended by Doctor Drake – seven out of the total of nine.'

'A little worrying,' said the senior surgeon, mopping blood from Steven's stitched-up left temple.

'Very,' said his junior partner, 'particularly bearing in mind that Doctor Drake is just one of a Rosedale total of six consultant psychiatrists.'

'So what are you thinking, then; what are you trying to say?'

'That I'm concerned, to say the very least.'

'That an operation like this one wasn't necessary?'

'I can't say for sure – I don't know the patient like a psychiatrist does – but it worries me somewhat . . .'

As Steven was wheeled to the sick bay to have fresh bandages and a fortnight of sedation and pain-killers and, last of all, removal of stitches, Luke Lloyd Evans happened to arrive upon the scene on the busy main corridor.

He looked very concerned and spoke with a curious uncertainty as to what might be going on. 'Is that Stevie Simms I see beneath those bandages?'

'It is,' spoke one of the nurses whose job it was to wheel patients on trolleys to the sanatorium.

Luke Lloyd Evans stared long and hard at the inert mummification before him, the stains of blood upon Steven's blonde hair. 'It's not what I think it is, is it? Surely not, but yet I dread . . .' he faltered.

45

'Correct. Straightforward frontal leucotomy,' said one of the stretcher-bearers. 'Just completed in theatre one, but no apparent side-effects discerned . . .'

'I should bloody hope not!' said Luke. 'And there's probably no prizes for guessing who the initial recommendations were made by . . .'

He paused in deep thought for a few seconds then said, 'I think that Bob Driscoll should be made aware, maybe the boss Ralph Johnson too . . .' Luke strode off down the busy, rather narrow, main corridor *en route* to Wing Eleven, the building where consultants' offices were located.

Bob Driscoll paced the room irritably, restlessly, angrily. 'I mean, is there any logic or scarce remaining remnants of a professional ethic in this place, or what? Since when does a Rosedale consultant like Drake have the dangerous arrogance of philistinism to personally select a second opinion?' He was really fuming now; Luke couldn't agree more.

'Usually it's a solicitor's domain, yes? A travesty of ethical responsibility and accountability to sidestep a patient's basic legal rights under the 1983 Act.'

Driscoll stopped his pacing and looked hard and straight at Luke. 'Yes, it's an incidence of malpractice, easily enough to be struck off a register for life. In some hospitals it would be instant dismissal!'

'But not so it seems here,' said a puzzled Luke.

'Because this place is the most disgraceful effrontery to health modernism, the worst place on this planet,' said Driscoll, resuming his impatient pacing.

'So,' said Luke, 'what now?'

'Ralph Johnson's suite at the very least,' barked Driscoll, ushering Luke towards the door and moving with him.

'I'm afraid to say that I'm by no means totally convinced,' said an intransigent Ralph. 'You can't convert me to side with your rather emotively charged views as a result of what is probably a quite justified leucotomy.'

'No disrespect, Ralph,' Bob interjected, 'but are you aware of the large absence of the actual justifications given in this particular case?'

'That's not really my department, though, is it Bob?' said a rather flippant objective Ralph Johnson. 'It's a matter for resort to the Patients Complaints Committee of the Quality Care Department, or if desired, the Mental Health Commission.'

'A bit too late though now, don't you think?' said Driscoll caustically.

'What does our psychologist feel about all of this?' said Ralph with general, if a little sarcastically tainted, interest.

'I have to side with Bob here, Ralph,' said Luke, speaking his mind clearly and firmly. 'If the closing years of this century have proclamations of democracy, fairness and care, then Rosedale must not be excluded from such ideas.'

'You're saying that our hospital rhetoric falls quite well short of reality, then?'

'It speaks for itself, I feel,' said a somewhat fatalistic Luke. 'In particular, over the last two or three years or so.'

'And to where or at what do you point the finger at what's gone wrong?' said Ralph attentively.

'Not so much "gone wrong", but rather "gone sour",' said Luke. 'The demise of notions of collective altruistic team-work, mutually recognised professional respect.'

Ralph spoke now with no derision in his voice, also it seemed a little bit fatalistic, resigned to unavoidable confrontation with fact. 'I agree, but is it really the likes of you or I to get the blame, the brunt of it all? Is it not out of our hands, out of our capacity to control? I feel damn certain that's so.'

Bob Driscoll again cut in angrily. 'So you're blaming the government health ministers for the way that people such as yourself effectively and directly manage day-to-day Rosedale policy?'

'No, no, no. Don't over react, Bob! It's a lot deeper than that, more complex. If we get grossly under-funded then we can't have any pulling power for the most efficient medical personnel, no attraction of the psychiatric cream . . .'

Luke spoke. 'To replace, I assume, the Doctor Drakes of this world?'

Driscoll had forced himself to cool down, despite his lack of agreement with what he saw as Ralph's nonplussed theoretical abstractedness. He had a feeling that Ralph was not only remote from reality of Rosedale, but human beings in a far broader sense. Although Bob had never actually voiced his feelings about Ralph's inappropriateness of position as Rosedale chief, he much awaited Ralph's not-too-distant retirement. Then Rosedale might be the phoenix to rise from its present pathetic sloppiness, its lethargic stupor of ashes, with new blood in the shape of a dynamic, committed replacement in the post. A realistic, above all, genuinely concerned medical director. Bob hoped such a day was not too far away.

Very unusual indeed. So rare was it in fact, that Dave Harrison would hardly ever be seen in a public telephone booth. But there again – it was absolutely essential to ensure strict confidentiality in this particular case. That being so, it was indeed a judicious move by Harrison not to make any calls to the *Mercury* via a Rosedale phone. The windows of the kiosk were steamed up, rivulets of condensation everywhere as Harrison made his furtive call. A rapid speaking, somewhat excitable voice rasped down the wires into his ear.

'*Mercury* newspapers,' said the female secretary. 'Your name, please . . .'

'Alan Green,' replied and lied Harrison. 'Could you perhaps locate a Jim Holland? Thank you,' he replied formally a little pleased at his subterfuge, his critical effort to cover all tracks seeming to work.

The phone crackled again with a slower drawl of a voice. 'Hullo, Jim Holland . . .'

'Right,' said Harrison. 'Alan Green's fictitious, but you'll understand I've to cover all possible contingencies – even with your own switchboard staff. By the way, I'm speaking from a public phone in town . . .'

'I see,' said Holland. 'Is this a preliminary to our rendezvous, or something new?'

'Both,' replied Harrison. 'And there's no need for either of us to adopt a taciturn attitude to one another; you'll find it food for thought what I'm about to divulge; interested or not?'

'Very. Fire away . . .'

'It's not some simple spilling of beans or a routine mediocre disclosure, much more than that . . .'

'A crusade? A serial story? What angle is it, and why?' Holland enquired absorbedly.

'That's the beauty of it, the jewel in the *Mercury* crown, so to speak,' rattled Harrison as he began to get in full flow. 'You see, it's the kind of stuff papers never ever are able to get – save by an actual break-in to Rosedale or bugging . . .'

'You mean it's quite personalized . . .'

'Oh, extremely, but that still misses the real beauty of it all . . .'

'I'm confused,' said Holland.

'Okay, it's like this; a disclosure of medical and legal reports upon an actual patient history with the inclusion of that same person's rehabilitation outings in the very public's midst!'

Jim Holland badly needed to think. This Harrison seemed weird – for so many equally weird reasons. Why should a professional employee, one ostensibly a carer or helper of patients' welfare, especially a social worker, be pursuing such a contradictory course. Surely, it not only utterly failed to add up, it was fundamentally irrational.

'You mean your motive is a Rosedale scandal exposed so as to get public and Health Department pressure to get Rosedale shut down, not any personal axe to grind about any particular person, right?'

'Yes. It's regrettable, the actual point of entry I've had to choose, to damage a patient's interests and future by giving you information on his case, but I saw no other way. In fact, I really love my patients, and in a roundabout, somewhat convoluted way, this will be to their long term advantage . . .'

'And you, for such views and motives, desire no personal payment?'

'None whatsoever . . .'

'Where do we meet?'

'I suggest a casual pub, Friday lunchtime. The Commercial would be fine.'

'One-thirty next Friday?'

'Fine. It should be interesting; what do you think?'

'Quite so; and excluded from other press, I take it?'

'Oh, most surely – this is the sole prerogative of the *Mercury*, make no mistake about that. One-thirty, Commercial, light lunch, future cessation of all contact, okay?'

'Okay,' agreed Holland, and then the line went dead. Harrison had said his piece.

Jim Holland sat in his stuffy, smoky little car during his lunch hour, chain-smoking, in deep, highly self-intriguing thought. Certainly Dave Harrison's mentality was itself open to doubt as to any firmness of morals. Even more strange was his actual grip upon his own sanity. Was it realistic to expect a leaking of an individual's case history would necessarily connect to far wider Rosedale alleged malpractices – and effect, for certain, a total closure? Holland saw such an impulsive line of reasoning as adopted by Harrison as extremely tenuous, a line of argument casting doubt upon mental powers of logic and reason. But still, whether the deal between Harrison and the *Mercury* was to Harrison's success of his high expectations was not the main issue in Jim Holland's mind. For Jim Holland had, it seemed, little option but to regardlessly persevere with his Rosedale investigation via Dave Harrison's convoluted strategy. For Rosedale was a formidable fortress of secrecy, and if Harrison was ignored, there seemed to be no other point of entry within. So, like it or not, Holland felt forced to proceed with a rather impulsive desperado of a morally twisted social worker.

Chapter Six

Born illegitimate was only the beginning of what was to be a downward slide into an abyss of depression. A state of acute mental morbidity, a moribund spiral which knew no limit, just infinite black depths. With his mother having died of tuberculosis when he was just three, his upbringing was undertaken by an unfeeling, domineering uncle and aunt. Then at primary and junior school, even early on at senior school, all the bullying, above all the malicious playground jibes and taunts of bastard, bastard, bastard! At fifteen, Colin Oakley had had enough, more than enough. So he plunged off a bridge to fall twenty feet to concrete below, only to be denied death, instead breaking both legs with spinal injuries. Then some social services department somehow latched onto Colin's lifestyle; an anxious, typical eleventh hour social worker concern which drew him into the widening catch-net of the ostensibly caring society. Fifteen years old, alone, lonely, unhappy – and long term it seemed – within the confines of Rosedale asylum.

There seemed to be no future. A tunnel never ending, a tunnel without light. Colin saw blackness at breakfast, mid-morning, all afternoon, throughout empty meaningless evenings, and all night long. Nothing could help his plight – not even the wisest of physicians, because it was too late. What had happened in the past, those early damaging experiences, powerfully choked all promise of anything remotely suggestive of a worthwhile future. Blackness. A day of pain, twenty-four futile hours of running away from a biography which had stamped upon him the seal of fate. A nomad, unable to have or find roots amongst a socially alien landscape. Only an existence of lifelessness, no bright beacons suggesting paths out of the pit, just an inexorable journey without signposts.

So many deluges of failures, faults, dilemmas, regrets, all began to reveal their mind-breaking futility of incompleteness as Colin felt them crystallizing all at once in his solitary bedroom at two o'clock in the chilly morning.

He'd managed to keep a razor hidden in a drawer of his room beneath layers of shirts. That razor blade was successfully seducing him now, it was saying 'take me, use me' and Colin was most surely in its destructive spell. Nobody about, no nurses and other patients all fast asleep. No one about at all; it was to be now and he must not botch up the job of self extinction. His tired head swam with turmoil, dizzy with depressive exhaustion; now was the time. He reached for that blade. Cutting deep he stifled his screams in his own body, fifteen tortured years old. He fell back upon the bed bleeding profusely, having severed a major artery. He had long lost consciousness as the white starched bed sheets took on a tragic colouration of deepest red. Nobody had, he felt, ever acknowledged his life with loving concern, and it seemed a cruel twist that his death, too, was an utterly solitary vigil; for he was not discovered in his cold lifelessness until ten o'clock the next morning.

At ten o'clock Rosedale was a clinical cauldron of pandemonium. Some *Mercury* reporters had somehow sniffed a little smoke of the suicide – much to the embarrassment of the upper echelons at Rosedale. Then there was the difficult job of pin-pointing responsibility of night-time staff observational failure. This was always so infuriatingly typical in a place like Rosedale: when something goes wrong in an institution and those up top blame their subordinates for supposedly not performing their job descriptions properly. The ward phone in the nursing staffs' office was ringing non-stop, a tired, hassled ward sister doing her very best to placate the victim's solicitors.

'I don't know,' was all Kim Hesketh could keep saying, 'I've only been on duty on this ward for two hours. I just don't know, I'm sorry . . .'

Photographers had to be called in to take shots of the actual room, the position of the emaciated fifteen-year-old and now dead bloody heap sprawled grotesquely upon the bed. Kim Hesketh had a thousand thoughts rushing through her swirling mind: that internal security would have to be immediately tightened up – all patients would have to be supervised whilst shaving, with all razors collected immediately afterwards, accounted for, then put under firm lock and key. Such a directive would come from the Rosedale upper management. Also, no doubt from now on, nightly observation by nursing staff would have to be stepped up, made more frequent. Quite simply – no patient must be allowed to kill themselves, or even attempt to do so any more. What annoyed Kim Hesketh, the ward sister, was that it was always the ward nurses who were first targets in the critical line of fire – despite it not usually being their fault. She would be told that she was not running her ward properly, that incidents like last night should never have been allowed to happen; certainly it would have negative repercussions as regards her chances of promotion in the future. And yet, she had not even been on the ward for three days and nights until this morning! She'd finished a four day shift of forty hours and simply taken her three days off, utterly oblivious to the sorts of goings on, or build up to such goings on as this latest incident. Yet, now it seemed she was to carry the can.

Ralph Johnson was fuming, his anger concentrated on why the suicide was not preventable by ward based night staff, plus a curious tone of an insistent solicitor who would not be easily fobbed off.

Such a situation lay upon Ralph's office desk after a bad night of chest pains with absolutely no sleep at all. His irritability rising by no means from this particular episode, but years upon years of what Ralph saw as a sloppy, ramshackle of anything even remotely resembling a psychiatric hospital. The objective should be a clear line of communication between all levels – administration, nursing, psychology, management, social work and other more specialised clinical areas. Nobody seemed to work together any longer. It was so atomised a team, a fragmentation of a crucially needed co-operative medical enterprise. Equally, no single individual seemed to be either responsible or accountable for their actions – always referring a matter to somebody else, some other level or department.

Perhaps this was why Rosedale rarely functioned to Ralph's satisfaction, to his much hoped for desire. There could in such an organisation be no good, wise, efficient grand plan – only a blueprint of continual set backs, hassles, dilemmas – many of these insoluble, at least so long as the public stigma of mad and bad loonies remained.

The incident of the previous night had just about put the lid on Rosedale's lack of efficiency, and simultaneously removed Ralph's lid of self control – he was so incredibly angry over a fifteen-year-old not having received the appropriate medical treatment, and therefore avoiding a terrible wastage of life.

Ralph twiddled with his pen; who, he thought, was actually responsible? Even more important, which individual medic was responsible for this specific tragedy? He reached for the phone.

'Sister Hesketh?' came a tired, female voice.

'Look,' Ralph barked, 'apart from being totally inadequate and incapable of even simply running your own ward, could you at least try and get one thing right!'

'What's that, Mr Johnson?'

'Tell me clearly, in no uncertain terms, who the most recent consultant was in the Colin Oakley care plan and, in particular, who authorised his medication?'

'Doctor Driscoll,' Kim replied, 'but a later intervention by a junior registrar, so that . . .'

Ralph Johnson cut her short. 'I'm not interested in junior bloody registrars! Who, I repeat, was the last actual fully qualified consultant?'

'As I said,' replied Kim, 'It was Doctor Driscoll, but then . . .'

'Thank you!' Ralph shouted down the phone. 'That's all I need to know.' He slammed down the phone, then dialled switchboard in reception.

'It's Ralph Johnson. Is Bob Driscoll on site? Have you seen him this morning?'

'No, sir, he's not arrived in hospital. Could I take a message?'

'Yes, you can. As soon as he shows his late mid-morning face, tell him I want to see him straightaway, in my office, okay?'

'Yes, sir,' came a timorous, very obedient reply.

'Oh, and there's another thing too,' Ralph irritably exclaimed in his rapid speech. 'Who, if anyone, is currently handling this suicide from an official clinical point of view?'

'I believe that Doctor Drake at this present moment is briefing Colin Oakley's solicitor and, as I am led to believe, one or two local pressmen.'

Ralph hung up and sat thoughtfully, then opened a window to dispel the office mustiness. No doubt Drake could give the press an adequate clinical speel tailored to their requirements of a simple tabloid formula and also keep it all played down a bit. Ralph wondered where Bob Driscoll might be and what he was doing, also how Drake was performing in fencing off concerns which hopefully would not materialise into damaging complaints, and in doing so, not damage further a teetering, wobbly Rosedale of which Ralph ultimately was responsible.

Clearly Drake was in his element. 'You see,' he said addressing a mini-audience of local media reporters and a couple of solicitors, 'it's all a question of clinical judgement . . .'

'At the right time, especially?' said a female television reporter.

'Exactly,' said a firm but confident Doctor Drake. 'But it is also a matter of being prepared to make a decision oneself, not rely necessary upon opinions of others, and crucially be fully prepared to have to shoulder such responsibilities, whatever the final outcome.'

'So,' said a solicitor in a blue striped suit, 'a matter not just of clinical professionalism with attendant responsibility, but crucially accountability as well?'

'Oh yes,' said Drake, 'most surely so. I've worked in psychiatry for many years and you get a feel for the actual nature of the job, an ability to size things up with a gut feeling, as well as being able to simply sum things up.'

'I see,' said another reporter. 'The job's demanding due to its uncertainty, its unpredictability of subject matter and resulting situations?'

'Yes, a good point that,' said Drake in a condescending congratulatory manner. 'It's essentially two things: subject matter, that is the actual patients and situations, and the patients' actual behaviour. Both are unknowns.'

'Which must be the reason why mistakes occur like this current suicide, unless medical personnel are sufficiently skilled and experienced to avoid such incidents,' said the solicitor.

'Yes, you've got it in one there,' said Drake, again rather patronizingly. 'I couldn't have expressed it better myself.'

'So, as regards Colin Oakley's state of mind,' said the solicitor, 'it had not been adequately probed in the preceding days leading up to such a tragic event, I take it?'

'No doubt that line of reasoning is the saddest part of this whole unhappy business,' said Drake in a hollow tone, waiting eagerly to be asked the biggest question of all, the one he wanted to be asked the most.

It came. The ultimate ego booster, and in full sight and hearing of important media and legal people. It was a brilliant opportunity to effectively negate any derogatory opinions or doubts held by some Rosedale medics about Drake's actual psychiatric competence, especially concerning powers of his clinical judgement and recommendations over recent months.

That blockbuster, pride-amplifying, status-soaring question. It was hovering upon the solicitor's lips, Drake waiting so patiently and fully prepared to be asked it, and answer it. Now it was asked and Drake must reveal no excitability or give any impression to these people of a rehearsed answer . . .

The solicitor spoke. 'This actual incident, Doctor Drake. Do you yourself, with your own particular powers of professional judgement, feel that had you been on call that you would have handled it differently?'

Here was Drake's springboard towards his own excellent prospects of a public relations stunt. He was going to really spin this one out and play it to his maximum advantage.

He spoke, his hands giving expression to his reply. 'First, I would have handled the whole affair very differently, and secondly, I feel that had that been the case then such a terrible tragedy could have been avoided . . .'

'How would you have actually handled it, Doctor Drake?' a reporter curiously asked, as all faces looked in mesmerised attention at Drake.

'Well, I'm led to believe,' said Drake with a machiavellian evasiveness, 'that for some days prior to the actual incident itself that a method of treatment had been prescribed by another consultant, a method that I personally would not have deemed appropriate.'

'What treatment did this other physician actually prescribe?' asked a solicitor seriously.

'Chemotherapy and only chemotherapy,' replied Drake succinctly.

'What's chemotherapy exactly?' continued the solicitor.

'Drugs,' replied Drake. 'A whole range exists for all sorts of different mental disorders. In this actual case I understand that anti-depressants in tablet form had been prescribed as the mode of alleviating a condition of a depressive neurosis, accompanied by some additional psychotic disturbance within the patient concerned.'

'So you feel that, in retrospect, it was a huge error on behalf of the other physician?'

'Obviously, it wouldn't be ethical for me to question the views or the course of action adopted by another consultant, but I still feel that it could have been handled both differently and most crucially of all, effectively. For if it had been so, then a fifteen-year-old could, perhaps, still be with us.'

Drake paused, took an intake of melancholy, lamentable breath and awaited the next few questions which he could easily anticipate and prepare answers for in advance. A good one came from one of the local evening news reporters, a little man with a rather reddish complexion and some patches of what appeared to be acne.

'So, Doctor Drake, you would not have prescribed drugs in this case, or chemotherapy, as you call it?'

'No. That would, I feel, have been far too mild or ineffective a preventative measure, bearing in mind the acuteness or severity of Colin's mental condition, which I understand was chronic.'

'So with a chronic state like Colin's, what would you have done?'

'ECT,' said Drake firmly, with all the conviction he could genuinely appear to muster. 'Electro-Convulsive Therapy, particularly good at curing acute bouts of a depressive psychosis from which Colin was suffering.'

'That's shock treatment then?' asked the solicitor.

'Yes, but I need to say here that there's a lot of myths about ECT which put fear in people's minds, when in actual fact, it is quite painless, and often with a severe depressive illness such as Colin's, it is quite simply the only effective treatment available.'

'So you would have given ECT?'

'Yes, and on a sessional basis, until clear indications of improvement were discerned by ward nursing staff, using appropriate methods of observations.'

The young reporter solemnly asked a question of Drake's general views about psychiatry as a profession and Drake's perception of it.

'It must be an extremely difficult and taxing job at times?'

'What? Psychiatry? Well, it's no garden of roses and calls for specialist skills in relating to something that consultants cannot even see: the patient's mind. In an ordinary general hospital it's far easier, a broken leg for instance can be clearly seen, treated and healed, but not so an afflicted mind. Hence the slow advance forward of my profession.'

'You must have been close to despair, then, over a tragedy like this present one.'

'Utterly shocked and shattered at such a loss of life, particularly when, as I believe, it could have been prevented.'

The solicitor, duped as he hopelessly was, could only look at Doctor Drake with admiration. Drake had radiated a highly infectious popularity, a caring charisma which could only continue to flourish in public and media opinion. Due to this little, but crucial, meeting, Drake's image was of a paternal angel watching over this hard world's unfairly mentally afflicted, wounded children.

The gathering now had a sad, almost silent, speechless atmosphere, as the solicitor drew it to a close. 'Thank you,' he said quietly. 'I don't think we need to ask you anything more, for it must obviously be creating you unhappiness, this entire terrible affair.'

There was a soft knock on Ralph Johnson's door. Ralph tore

his eyes from piles of paperwork, and looked up, strained and rather annoyed.

'Come in,' he brusquely said.

'I gather you wished to see me urgently,' said a weary, pasty-faced Driscoll. 'No doubt concerning what lots of people have mentioned to me since I set foot in reception ten minutes ago . . .'

'Sit down,' said Ralph pointing to a deep leather chair.

'There's no need for what I suspect might be a confrontation,' said Bob.

'I'll be the judge of that,' said Ralph. 'Now, what's all this turning up at eleven o'clock business eh? You criticise Doctor Drake for all sorts of alleged inefficiencies, but at least he's actually here, available . . .'

'Doctor Drake has probably not missed a full night's sleep or had an onset of flu,' countered Driscoll assertively.

'I see,' said Ralph a little bit more mellowed and reasonable, his sting partly tempered by Bob Driscoll's explanation.

Driscoll continued, determined to give what he strongly felt was a good side, his side of the story. 'Yesterday, I was here at seven-thirty, and didn't leave till well gone seven-thirty in the evening, right!' He continued slowly but firmly. 'Then when I arrive here feeling dizzy and hot like my head's about to burst, I get superficial feedback from some spotty clerk in reception about a press meeting and Drake's goings on, with full reference to me, with untold implications in my uninformed absence or capacity. What do you think about that?' Bob Driscoll was now in full angry flow. 'I am also led to believe that your superwoman of a number two in charge, Miss White should have been the one to let me know about this. How do you feel about that?'

'How *should* I feel?' said a by now, rather demoralised Ralph.

Driscoll took a huge intake of angry breath pointing his finger at Ralph. '*How should you feel?* I'll tell you, shall I? You should feel that, more and more, this place is a circus, an arena of "balls-ups" and of totally pathetic characters of one brilliant best-seller of a farce!'

'Have a coffee,' said a tired, almost defeated medical director.

'I prefer orange, the state my throat's in,' said Driscoll. 'And where, might I ask, is your super-efficient deputy? Immersed in superfluous paperwork no doubt, or anything that's not useful . . .'

'Oh, now that's uncalled for,' said Ralph protectively. 'Well below the belt. Do you wish me to try and contact her with a view to patching up today's shambles?'

'I damn well do, but there's no guarantee I can give you an armistice, she's so bloody aloof . . .'

'What from?' asked Ralph earnestly.

'Everything and anything relevant,' Bob replied.

'What's relevant?' said Ralph rather stupidly.

'Look!' said Driscoll, 'I'm not going to blow my top here and now again; just let me say that Suzy is a good case study of one with a chronic pathology who cannot, *will not*, acknowledge reality.'

'Reality, meaning being involved with others?' said Ralph, a little like a gawping student.

Driscoll gave a forced smile, simultaneously forcing his anger away. It was useless to keep explaining to the Rosedale number one, for Ralph was as remote from his designated job as was Suzy White; it seemed to Driscoll that both Ralph and Suzy had never heard of something called 'other people', their fellow human beings. He drank a large glass of orange in one continuous gulp and headed for Suzy White's office. He didn't bother to knock, opened the door and strode right in.

'I do exist, you know,' said Driscoll as Suzy White looked up slowly from her word processor, a little confused and astonishingly largely unaware of Bob's sense of urgency.

'Something wrong?' she said slowly and naïvely.

'Yes, very,' Bob exclaimed.

'What?' she asked, puzzled.

'You,' Bob said.

'Me? How?'

'By spending a fifty-two week annual holiday in your ivory tower with your computer and its thousands of bits of paper; anything but other people – like me.'

Suzy put her hands to her head in realization of what she perceived was a slight error on her part. 'Oh, I'm sorry Bob, it's about this morning's goings on, isn't it?'

'Damn right!' said Bob looking her straight in the eyes. 'It's just like I said a few moments ago, I do exist you know . . .'

'Sorry. Of course you should have been informed, immediately, by me personally. I guess it's all this new privatisation stuff I've been wading in. So snowed under with new appointments, nurse grading procedures, new departments, etcetera; take it from me Bob, it completely slipped my mind.'

It completely slipped her mind! Good grief! thought Bob. A young man dead, an interview with the press he'd not even been aware of, though definitely should have been, and now all and sundry feeling it was primarily his faulty diagnosis which triggered the tragedy. He felt very hot both through wrath and an insidious setting in of influenza.

Bob looked into her powdered face with its layers of make-up. He spoke decisively to her and she could not keep meeting his furious gaze. 'Suzy, the event of last night was something harsh, insensitive and unprofessional too, don't you agree? It's the nineteen-nineties not the eighteen-eighties . . .'

'That sort of talk is completely unfair . . .'

'Well, what happened last night wasn't exactly fair either, was it?'

'Bob,' she said at length, 'you can't take on the problems of the entire world's mental health single-handed.'

'True,' Bob said, 'quite true, but at least I try.'

'Meaning what, exactly?'

'That you dismally fall short in your capacity of relevance.'

'So you're saying I'm irrelevant?'

'I'm not saying anything except the truth,' Bob said, turning his back on her and walking out of her untidy, paper-cluttered office.

'What is there to say about last night and this morning?' said Luke, as he and Bob sipped their coffees and took deep puffs on their cigarettes.

'Not a lot,' said Bob, his shirt wet with perspiration. 'I'll shoot off in a minute to my office and get some aspirins from my case. My headache's killing me.'

'Why not quite legitimately go off sick?' said Luke, concern showing in his astute eyes.

'Too much to do which can't wait,' he said, 'can't possibly be delayed or deferred.' He put down his coffee only half-finished, regretting having drank any, wishing he's simply drank a pint of cold water instead.

Luke watched him slowly traverse the staff canteen feeling a hell of a lot of sympathy for not simply a brilliant psychiatric colleague, but much more important, a best friend.

Chapter Seven

Bob Driscoll sat in his office watching the day die. Lengthening shadows of a miserable winter afternoon decided to impose themselves upon paint-flaking walls of the office. An untidy room, the contents of which Bob regarded as well-nigh irrelevant to the actual nature of the job. A 'razzmatazz' paraphernalia of electrical equipment – computer, word processor, fax machines and lots of other gadgetry he had so little time for, and hardly ever used. He reflected upon what he saw as diversions, side-tracks to what had always been the essence of his job. It seemed to be a confusing morass of too many people on the Rosedale pay-roll, all bumping into one another, unable to any longer address themselves to the patients.

Bob Driscoll lit a cigarette, his dose of flu improving since he'd seen Ralph Johnson a few days ago. Bob was a thinker, always alert to hospital malpractice, inefficiency, human resource wastage, issues of incompetence, neglect by his colleagues. Such thoughts directly concerned him now with a rapidly darkening late afternoon, the grey atmosphere allowing his imagination full nostalgic rein. For instance: of course he'd love to quit his Rosedale post, get away from lots of idiots he disliked – those he saw as totally immobile and sterile of a progressive psychiatric approach, such as Ralph or Suzy White. But then came the dilemma – if he decided to say goodbye to Rosedale he'd leave a lot of patients behind he had lots of time for, wished to help and then recommend for release. No matter how many torpedoes of a stupefying inertia had hit and were damaging Rosedale, he couldn't bear to leave such a beleaguered sinking ship.

He stubbed out a cigarette and pondered over the next few hours as to whom to see. Either subconsciously or perhaps even consciously he felt a tiny spark of a sexual thrill. Danny – dark, young, smooth. Danny – young, pure, soft. Danny – never ever to be in the slightest way de-spoiled by the Rosedale machine. Bob would see him today – but first of all an important thing to also do – a visit to sick bay to see the follow-up state of patient Steve Simms, an involuntary mental victim to a surgeon's knife, via a recommendation of a Drake-like philistinsim.

'Do you remember me, my voice, my face?' Doctor Driscoll asked with utmost attentiveness, genuine concern.

In Simm's empty shapeless stare there was not simply a vacancy but a far worse expression of vagrancy, a wanderer now and forever within the wilderness of his own confined world. Driscoll looked at Simm's forehead, a rather ugly scar, and a remaining bandage which was a little bloodstained and needed changing. Driscoll wondered, could Simms actually speak?

'How are you feeling? Any pain?' Driscoll asked slowly and clearly. At that, Simms' eyelids seemed to flicker a sense of recognition of another person. Driscoll, who was earnestly looking for such signs put his hands upon Simms' arm, again speaking deliberately, very slowly and clearly. 'Do you smoke?'

'Yes,' came the delayed reply as Driscoll lit a cigarette and passed it to a rather motionless Simms, whose damaged nervous system made such actions slow and lethargic.

'I shall be coming to see you quite a lot and to discuss plans for moving you out to a better, nicer place, away from here,' Bob said.

And yet immediately after having just said those exact words of encouragement to Simms, Driscoll felt utterly stupid for having said such a thing. For after all, Bob Driscoll thought, it's a bit late now to talk about any improvement of this poor sod's quality of life or a future, after the leucotomised crippling damage, so terribly afflicted upon him recently.

'Another place? A flat? A home of my own?'

Driscoll felt like crying, and was very much on the verge of a hysterical outburst of grief. For he knew only too painfully well that prior to Simms having had the leucotomy, a flat or place of his own could have well been quite a realistic proposition, a reasonable request for the medical team to seriously consider, to no doubt materialise. But not now, no longer. Particular constraints upon Simms' scope of freedom most definitely put on him a label of maximum dependency, and hence, a collective residence to live in, not a place of his own. A supervised hostel, accommodation for collectively broken dependents, all judged to possess insufficient mental faculties of independence, decision making, above all, responsibility.

So as Bob talked about things to Simms that would never be, he inwardly cursed himself for making empty promises, dreams that would never materialise. But it was not so easy to try the converse, that is, for Driscoll to tell Simms the truth. For such a realistic revelation would be shattering, a disclosure of a future little better than being damned.

As Doctor Driscoll stood up to go and leave patient Simms to rest and smoke a cigarette, Driscoll couldn't help but think and know that Simms' life was from now on largely hopeless, a futile future, a life in many ways already over.

But on the contrary, Ward Fourteen was an occasion, a place of psychological nirvana, a palace containing a young pharaoh in the immortal form of Danny Broughton. Bob closed the bedroom door telling a nurse that he wished no intrusions, and not to be on any account disturbed. From Bob's face drained away any previous harrowing days of anguish, of any lines of screwed-up intensity, any stressful craters or pockets of pain. Bob Driscoll could now relax, the sight before him more therapeutic than any relaxation programme available.

It was good, so mind expanding, so mentally unwinding to be in love. Right now Gill meant almost nothing at all, but Danny's virgin fresh, undefiled white skin contrasting with medium length jet black hair, was something you could only liken to a beauty capable of transcending the mortal world. For Bob, Daniel was the light of the world, or more precisely, light of Bob's mind. Already the mistiness of eyes was going away, that preceding visitation to Simms, the sharpness of shocked horror was diminishing, anger receding. All the last weeks' turmoil and fury, upset and rancour was in retreat, for now Daniel's body had banished such a plague from Bob's mind. Slowly Bob leaned forward and kissed Daniel ever so softly and delicately upon the forehead, careful and protectively concerned not to awaken him.

Daniel Broughton: a very young, magnificent king. A timeless, priceless, precious entity which must never be eclipsed by Rosedale's constellation of disfiguring therapies. No Drakes must ever have Daniel's vulnerable flesh in their clutches, their so called 'treatment' or therapy programmes. No electric shocks or steel scalpels for this particular one, this kind of Bob Driscoll's adoration. Bob kissed him again, softly, this time upon the white sleeping lips. It was an incredibly dangerous game for Doctor Driscoll to play. A breach of professional ethicality which could only, if detected, have the shattering outcome of instant dismissal. A striking-off forever from the medical register with utmost humiliation to follow. Bob knew all such pitfalls, but as he pressed his mouth upon Daniel's sweetly sleeping face, he really couldn't give a damn.

A sharp violently unwelcome knocking upon the bedroom door ended a dream Bob was still in the middle of, fully enjoying, and didn't want to so soon end. It was like being woken up in the best bit of a pleasurable, secretive dream, and Bob was very annoyed. Quickly disengaging and standing up quickly, he angrily confronted the nurse. 'I said on no account was I to be disturbed!'

'I'm really sorry,' she said, 'but it's the number one who wants you immediately. He says something's cropped up; he says it can't wait. I am sorry sir . . .'

'Okay,' said Driscoll, casting a last glance at his motionless, still sleeping god. 'I'll go and see Ralph, but it had better be bloody important.'

'I feel quite sure that it is,' said the timorous young red-head of a junior staff nurse, letting Bob Driscoll off the ward.

'About bloody time!' rasped Ralph Johnson. 'Where in God's name have you been? I've had people looking high and low everywhere for you . . .'

'There's such a thing reserved for all human beings,' said Bob dryly. 'It's called a little bit of privacy, a bit of autonomy, a right to at least some independence.'

'Well,' said Ralph, 'I'm very glad you've just said that, because now I'm going to deflate your ego, take the wind out of your independent sails.'

Bob's face perhaps betrayed the slightest sign of a concerned sense of disquiet. 'Go on then,' he said, sitting in one of the deep leather chairs and lighting a cigarette.

'You've created a bit of a stir,' Ralph said, thrusting a newspaper across the desk in front of Bob's eyes. 'There's not a lot about you personally, but I still think it'll be of some interest to you.'

Before even starting to read, Bob blew out cigarette smoke in exasperation. 'You do realise it wouldn't be like this if that press and Drake session hadn't occurred.'

'Maybe so,' said Ralph fatalistically as Bob continued.

'And that you Ralph, could have prevented that press meeting actually taking place, in your capacity as Rosedale number one . . .'

'But can't you see, Bob,' Ralph explained earnestly, 'if I'd refused the press entry it would only have exacerbated the situation, made them more suspicious, even more vigilant . . .'

'So you suggest, then, that Rosedale adopts an open-door policy, that press or media more generally can just drop in on us any time?'

'Now you're being a bit silly. You fail to see my actual position.'

'Well, if you're trying to say that you're hemmed in from all sides with no room for manoeuvre, then your persistence with your actual job is questionable, Ralph.'

'Meaning what, exactly?'

'That a medical director is a leader, or should at least try to be; not to sit on the fence, but actually move things about, direct people; not just keep a frightened head in the sand . . .'

'That's enough!' Ralph snapped. 'You're saying I should refuse press entry and all enquiries, so that they will dub Rosedale a secret Auschwitz? Then press stories would no longer be local but national, would blow Rosedale and all of us wide open. Is that what you think I should do? Fuel suspicion, and in so doing, make the Rosedale future ten times worse? Try putting yourself in my position, Bob, in my shoes. Can you think of many options, any good workable alternatives? I for one can't, and I'm damn certain, neither can you.'

Bob Driscoll looked pitifully across the desk at a wizened, ineffectual, almost broken, late middle-aged figure, one who had taken a post which was most surely a mistake. The Rosedale power hierarchy was so wobbly, so insecure. The primary reason was that the leader was not a leader – did not, could not lead – only pathetically delegate, and this unprofessional lethargy was crippling the entire hospital.

'And I suppose that, even after this total "balls-up" your views upon Doctor Drake's impeccability are still unchanged, yes?'

'I don't think we need to be pointing the finger at people like Drake,' Ralph insisted, stubborn in his resolve as ever. 'It's a problem, I feel, not of an actual consultant psychiatrist, but nursing staff who run the actual wards.'

So once again, Ralph was deflecting blame from himself, projecting it onto others; so in this case, nursing staff who he had probably never even bothered to meet or certainly not even considered approaching about the recent suicide of Colin Oakley. Bob Driscoll felt he had spent the past half hour or so talking to a stubborn, immature, unreasonable child in the shape of a Rosedale medical director. There seemed little point in listening to much more of such infantile nonsense, blindness to reason.

Driscoll put the paper back onto Ralph's cluttered desk and said, 'So you'd like me to go and give some ward nursing staff a good telling off, a good grilling about their apparent incompetence over this recent suicide?'

'Yes,' said Ralph. 'Give them a really good broadside about patient neglect and a warning that if there's a repeat tragedy, their very jobs will be on the line . . .'

Bob didn't say anything to Ralph about the banality of sacking, or threatening to sack, nursing staff, despite it not being in any way a nursing staff problem or target of blame. As Driscoll left the office he couldn't help but feel a strange, angry sensation within himself, of a capacity to exact violence.

Bob Driscoll greeted Kim Hesketh, the ward sister, with a broad but serious kind of facial expression. 'I've been sent here direct from Ralph to try and tell you off.'

'Tell me off?'

'That's what I'm supposed to be doing, but don't panic, Kim, I'm fully aware it was out of your hands.'

'Indeed so,' said Kim. 'I wasn't even on duty when the actual incident occurred.'

'Who was then?' enquired Driscoll, 'and what were staffing levels like, that day, that night?'

'We, as per usual, were chronically under-staffed. Some off

sick, some on leave. We were operating a virtual skeleton crew.'

'And the number of patients was what?' Bob asked.

'Thirty-two,' replied Kim. 'We had a day-time staff–patient ratio of three staff to effectively supervise thirty-two patients.'

Bob took an intake of surprised breath. 'I can't believe that,' he said. 'How on earth can three staff adequately perform all essential clinical duties for thirty-two patients?'

'It was even worse than that,' Kim exclaimed, 'for there was only one actual qualified nurse on the night shift, the other two are still training in a student enrolment capacity.'

'So you mean that observation levels would have been impossible to adequately perform, due to both low staff numbers and lack of training and qualified staff?'

'Absolutely,' Kim asserted, 'and the night time medications had to be given by that one solitary qualified nurse alone, due to students not being allowed to hand out drugs; only qualified nurses can do that.'

'What an abysmal state of affairs,' Bob said. 'And the staffing levels, having been decided by Administration, it wasn't a failure of any medics at ward level, especially not nursing staff.'

'That's it in a nutshell,' professed a weary, strained Kim Hesketh. 'All staffing levels, all shifts, numbers, the amount of "qualifieds" are all decided in advance by Admin's Allocation Department.'

'So you and the other nursing colleagues had no say in the matter, and couldn't influence what you could well have anticipated would be a very risky situation?'

'Yes, and what in fact turned out to be so risky as to lead to an actual fatality – the impossibility of observation being satisfactory that particular night and hence, a none preventable death.'

Kim stood silent, aware that a storm was inexorably on the mental health horizon; a hurricane would soon be on course. Its ugly brunt would be felt then by so many panicking pathetic figures who had actually created the storm, had engineered their own destruction. Bob and Kim walked slowly down the corridor, silent and sad.

Chapter Eight

Dave Harrison was already on his third pint whilst Jim Holland was still sipping his first.

'As a rule, I don't usually like midday drinking,' said Holland, peering through the smoke and digging his fingers into a packet of crisps. 'Makes me sometimes feel a bit sick.'

'Depends, I suppose, on what you've been doing,' said Harrison. 'And on how thirsty you are.'

'Not the most spacious of pubs is it?' said Holland. 'A bit of a poky little dive.'

'If you think that, then you wouldn't appreciate this place at night – you wouldn't get a seat and you wouldn't be able to swing a cat,' commented Harrison. 'But all the same, I like this little haunt – used to come here in my student days.'

'Underage, obviously,' said a well knowing Holland.

'Yes,' grinned Dave Harrison. 'Only problem was, I always looked far too young. It was a difficult exercise of good lying.'

'And masquerading as mature, like lots of other "A" Level spotty whizz kids I suppose?' said Holland.

'Well, what the hell,' added Harrison, 'we all do it, don't we?'

'Do we?' pressed Holland. 'I didn't, didn't have either enough cash or alcoholic inclination.'

Harrison paused then ruefully said, 'A bit odd that; I always thought of a press reporter dashing around, fag in mouth, living on coffee, lager, and pockets stuffed with notebooks and Biros.'

'Well, I can't speak for others, but that's certainly not me,' said Holland. 'It doesn't pay to hold too many stereotypes.'

'Doesn't it?' questioned Harrison. 'I always thought a newspaper's success thrived upon them.'

'Upon what?'

'Stereotypes, stock images, standard formulas.'

'Perhaps, but again, I've never operated that way. Still, maybe I'm a hypocrite.'

'How?' Harrison asked, intrigued by Holland's idiosyncratic dialogue.

'Because, as recently as this week, I had a classic, firm stereotype image of yourself, a typical social worker – corduroys, beard, thick turtle-neck jumper and half-moon glasses.'

'Have I disappointed you then?' grinned Harrison, who possessed no such physical or material adornments.

'To be ruthlessly honest, yes!' laughed Holland. 'You've spoilt my long established, grand image of all things social work is. My mental picture is in ruins!'

'So as you just said, best not to presuppose,' added Harrison, draining his third pint and lighting his pipe.

'But *that* definitely is a classic part of a social worker's survival kit!'

'What, a pipe?'

'Oh yes, down to a tee!' said Holland. 'And besides, we've been chatting for a good twenty minutes now about everything except the actual matter concerning us. Do you think the ice, our ice, is now broken?'

'It's well and truly broken,' said Dave. 'Before we begin, though, can I get you another drink, a half even?'

'No,' said Holland emphatically, staring down at Harrison's briefcase. 'I suppose it's in there?'

'What, the stuff you're interested in?'

'Maybe even fascinated in,' added Holland. 'This is the first real break the *Mercury*'s ever had, at least as regards strict confidentiality busting.'

'And to remain strictly confidential too as regards its source, okay?'

'You have my word on that,' said Holland, as Harrison passed him a large, fat brown envelope. Holland put it in his own briefcase and added, 'So I presume it's all here, no need for me to be taking notes or anything?'

'It's all there,' said Harrison, beads of perspiration beginning to surface upon his forehead, his face slowly reddening with the effects of the alcohol.

'I need fresh air,' said Holland, stubbing out a cigarette, his slightly glazed eyes focusing upon the wet beer mats on the copper-topped tables.

'Do you ever come here on a social basis?' asked Harrison.

'Only when I have an appointment with social workers,' commented Holland. 'In fact, I'd have preferred to have met you in the park, walk my lunch off, and get deeper into things with you.'

'Like what?' asked a slightly apprehensive Dave Harrison.

'Oh, there's no cause for concern, it's just a few little puzzles intriguing me about yourself.'

'Such as?'

'Well, you seem to have skirted around, or touched upon what, for lack of a better word, could be described as my morality – my puritan stance about alcohol in excess or what I do socially. Which leads me to throw a question towards you . . .'

'I know. I know exactly what you're thinking and about to say. Namely, why should I seem to be betraying the very ethics of my humane profession. Yes?'

'Yes,' said Holland, 'particularly when your avowed objective of a successful Rosedale shut-down may not necessarily occur.'

'No,' said Harrison, 'maybe not, but it could do plenty of "good damage", hurt those up top, let them sweat a bit, make them aware Rosedale's not a bed of happy roses.'

Jim Holland was more than just intrigued, he was stupefied as he looked deep into the pockets, hollows, shadows and the twisted lines of Dave Harrison's face. For after all, Jim reasoned to himself, why couldn't Dave Harrison have tried one of several alternative ways to draw a critical public eye to Rosedale? Simply to telephone a newspaper's head office, disclose juicy newsworthy data, remain anonymous – that could perhaps have just as well done the trick. Jim Holland, although resolved to go in hard, as Frank Farley his boss suggested, still had a tiny pang of moral guilt about a psychologically uneasily feeling of conspiracy.

For a good half hour, Jim Holland sat smoking in his rusty red car, pondering over his dinner hour liaison; he was itching to open the envelope he had furtively been given. Yes, of course he'd go ahead with it all, milk it to the maximum, a powerful spotlight to reveal Rosedale hospital as a secretive, obscene place, which indeed it seemed. In fact, it might even be a ten times better story it Holland were to double-cross Harrison and print an article about Harrison's role. A story hinging around a possible angle of Rosedale containing resentment from within. A subversion in its own ranks, a senior social worker to have actually tried, as Harrison effectively had done, to cripple the institutional management by adverse publicity; to expose the classified case-history of a patient, a helpless patient under Harrison's actual confidential care. What a blockbuster of a story that could be, and Jim Holland was excitably thinking of just such a ploy. But then it could perhaps get convolutedly difficult with Rosedale taking legal action, maybe against the *Mercury*. A hornets' nest could be stirred up, and Holland's strategy massively and badly backfiring upon him. That could indeed be the irony: a whiplash which could so easily see him fired, out of his *Mercury* office, out of a career. All that due simply to a greediness of wanting the biggest, best story.

Within minutes of entering Rosedale's plush Social Work

Department, the ticking of a psychological time bomb had ended; it had exploded with maximum impact and damage inside Dave Harrison's head.

What had happened was a once-in-a-million situation which had occurred upon his arrival back to work in the late afternoon. His alcohol reddened face had turned deathly white as a junior colleague greeted him with the news of the recently sad tragedy of Colin Oakley. The budding junior social worker was a little worried at Dave's reaction when he said that he wished to be alone 'to sort something urgent out'. What Dave Harrison meant by that his junior colleague didn't quite know, but still left the office to take a mid-afternoon break.

The once-in-a-million possibility had arrived – in the form of sweetest revenge from Rosedale hospital, which he hated. A bit of a Guy Fawkes who wanted to blow up something but botched up the job. It was truly amazing: not only *what* had happened, but *how* it had so unpredictably happened – and to Harrison's cost. For out of a possible five hundred confidential case notes of Rosedale psychiatric patients to choose from and put in a sealed envelope and present furtively to Jim Holland in a pub, Dave Harrison had chosen those of Colin Oakley, now a very dead man. Such legal and clinical documents Harrison had quite coolly and surreptitiously photocopied four days ago in his office, placed them in a large envelope, and gone off home for a few days, taking the envelope with him.

Perhaps if Holland had opened that envelope in the pub it would have been a very different outcome – Holland would have been able, in Harrison's presence, to easily recall the recent Rosedale suicide and immediately tell Harrison who was hitherto unaware of it. But such a merciful alternative scenario had, to Harrison's cost, not happened. Instead the picture was, for Dave Harrison, a very black one. He shuddered to think of what Jim Holland must think of him right now – a massive professional practical joker, or maybe far worse, a more scathing description?

Harrison dreaded such contemplation, transferring his thoughts to future reprisals – from Holland, his pleasant, albeit one-off drinking partner of a couple of hours before.

Holland did not know of Harrison's lack of knowledge about Oakley's death, and therefore would come to utterly despise Harrison, feeling betrayed into having accepted the case notes of a dead patient, which was useless material for a potentially newsworthy article. Of this, Harrison was also crushingly aware. In fact it was this last particular point that would anger Holland the most. Dave Harrison, head still buried in his wet hot hands, wondered just what Jim Holland must be thinking, feeling right now . . .

Jim Holland could not be feeling any more worse. An understatement was a good description to describe the sense of humiliation, fury, being cheated, which filled his thoughts. Why, he pondered, trust a sloppy, slovenly verbose clown as he in fact had done? A circus star attraction with letters after his name to show he'd read obscure airy fairy social policy books? But this was only half of the source of Holland's nauseated infuriated state. He sat chain-smoking in a room of a large building of Mercury Newspapers Ltd – not his own office, but that of his ever-vigilant superior. As Holland stared at the documents of Colin Oakley strewn about the desk in front of him, he felt unable to say anything useful, with regard to his defence. Frank Farley's darting, deep brown eyes suddenly, with frightening force, focused upon Holland, bore into him.

Farley spoke, unable to contain his irritation any longer.

'Stupid. I mean, you're really stupid, a pratt. A paper like ours should have the utmost shame. A real pratt. None of this could, by any stretch of the imagination, be possibly any more stupid. Can you deny that? No, you can't. You daft bugger. Can't you see the wood for the trees? Sometimes I ask myself if there's any point at all talking to you, even bothering to help; it's like trying to teach a five-year-old! I mean – for pity's sake –

why didn't you think it over beforehand, or bother to at least ask that nutter of a social worker-cum-parasite who the actual patient was?'

Holland spoke. 'I should have opened the envelope in the pub, in his presence, yes I know . . .'

'You should have done a hell of a lot more, *much* more than that. You shouldn't have even remotely contacted a social worker in the first place. He must be having one very great laugh at you now, sold you well and truly down the river, one which I'm very tempted to let you drown in . . .'

'What do you mean?' questioned a rather apprehensive Holland.

'To be sacked now, on the spot, and by God do I mean that!'

'No bluffing, Frank?'

'Absolutely deadly serious; fired forever from this paper. If you want to pack it in and resign then just bloody-well say so! It's not just me; quite a lot of comments are buzzing around these offices about you, and I'm embarrassed to have to keep making silly apologies to keep your reporter calibre above water. Like I said, I'm very tempted just to let you drown.'

It was perhaps, in a way, the fault of nobody in particular, of no actual individual. Although Jim Holland was absolutely convinced that Harrison had played a practical joke – something which was not in fact so – that was not the line of conversation Holland now was indulging in. The Harrison–Holland issue of severe confusion was essentially circumstantial and a private matter, not the topic Holland was discussing at the immediate moment, desperate to salvage his credibility for Frank Farley. For although there was obviously a connection between the two issues, Farley considered them as quite separate. What he now wished to hear from Holland might, if satisfactory, let Holland off the hook and keep him on the staff. For Farley didn't really give a damn about some two-bit weirdo of an informant of a social worker, but cared very much about his own staff's journalistic competence. Hence, Holland was almost sitting an oral examination as Frank patiently, but very seriously, listened.

Jim Holland stated the situation very neatly, about the way stories of a dead mental patient are worthless to print, even detrimental for a tabloid. What member of the public could sadistically read about the criminal record of a patient who has just tragically and sadly killed himself? No matter how vivid or sensational Colin Oakley's legal transgressions once committed, no matter how bizarre the reports upon his Rosedale psychiatric history, there is no titillation or sensationalism in reading a press article of such things, when that very person concerned is publicised as a tragic case of suicide.

Holland had it, knew he was in the clear, that Frank would give him another, although maybe a last, chance.

'Am I talking straight?' asked Holland. 'Do I make some sense, or am I now out on my ear?'

'Sense, Jim,' Farley replied, 'you're not out on your ear; but above all, for God's sake, think about this Rosedale mess as a lesson, a learning exercise lifelong, and especially how to still achieve our goal.'

'You mean I shouldn't abandon Rosedale as an angle?'

'No, never. It's an extremely good line to follow up; just try to think and investigate it successfully. Then *we* are a success, yes?'

'Yes,' uttered a slightly confused Jim Holland, noticing that it was 'we'. The 'we' from Frank implying that Jim do all the work and sweat, whilst Frank cream a lion's share of any glory of pay offs from resulting success.

A bitterly cold winter's evening saw Jim Holland sitting in his apartment in twilight, very deep in reflective thought. His career, in fact his future - certainly anything resembling a worthwhile future - hinged upon his actions over the next few days. He knew that vital weak spot of Rosedale penetration. Perhaps the only way in, but if it went in any way wrong, then it could prove so extremely costly – the brunt of it borne by himself. Yet he had no choice, no alternative; there was apparently no way out of the predicament he'd unwittingly put himself in.

Jim Holland reached for the phone and dialled Rosedale reception. As usual, a cool feminine voice asked for his identification and who he wished to speak to. Pleasantly and calmly, but in quite a forthright manner, he stated an alias name and bogus status of personal friend.

'You are a professional colleague?' the switchboard clerk asked.

'No, just a close away-from-work contact.' Holland was relieved she asked no further questions as he heard a pause of a few intermittent bleeping sounds.

'And you desire to speak to whom?' came the calm but business-like voice.

'Bob Driscoll,' said Holland, rather matter of factly, no strain in his voice.

'Bob Driscoll,' came a rather tired voice. 'Who's speaking please?'

Jim Holland was living dangerously right now, had to get it right. 'Is this conversation between only you and I, Bob?'

'Yes, who is speaking?'

'Jim Holland. This is extremely difficult to explain but I feel that I can assist you and I too can get out of a bit of a trap unscathed. Don't put the phone down on me please, at least till you've listened to what I've got to say.'

'You're a newspaper reporter?'

'A professional journalist, one who has a lot of empathy for you after your undeserved tarring and feathering of recent days, via a bit in my paper, by a certain Doctor. Is it a Doctor Blake or Drake?'

'It's Drake, although I can't see why you are choosing to contact me personally.'

'Because there's no option, not for me and, I sense, not for you either.'

'I still can't see my role in this. Why me?'

'I gather from various sources you'd like to put a lot right within that place, within its crumbling walls; if not exactly a radical, might I sense you're a rather keen reformist? This is, as I said, so difficult over the phone. Above all, this is no hoax, Doctor Driscoll, it's *bona fide* real; can we meet? I've a lot of things to discuss and I repeat, it's no hoax.'

Bob Driscoll breathed in and out strongly for several moments. It seemed ages until he rather nervously spoke. 'I'm not at all certain about all of this suddenly dropping onto me, but the way things are going here – to virtual rack and ruin – I believe there's something maybe in this, in what you say.'

'It *is* genuine, and in total confidence. I tell no fiction, only useful fact, useful for both of us. Do you know a quiet place?'

'I think that so long as it's far away from Rosedale it doesn't really matter if a place is quiet. In fact a busy café of anonymous people might be a better venue, a better ploy.'

'Do you know such a spot?'

Bob said quite surely on the knowledge founded upon six years of experience that he knew of just such a place. 'It's a little café close to the town centre; you probably know it, it's one of a fast food chain.'

'Reggie Carrero's?'

'That's the one,' said Bob. 'Let's say eight tomorrow evening at Reggie's, okay?'

'I know the place well,' said Holland, who happened to also frequent that particular place. 'Eight's fine with me.'

'Eight it is then,' said Bob and put the phone down, wondering what he might, for good or maybe bad, be letting himself into now.

Jim Holland wasn't as bright as Bob Driscoll, but was still hoping, even practically praying, that it would come off and bear fruit; only twenty-four hours later both desperados of circumstance would know. A browbeaten, worn-out doctor and a worried reporter living on thin ice; both casualties of their destinies which were not of their own making.

Chapter Nine

Nothing had changed. The plastic forks and spoons; coffee spills on formica tables; the pervasive odour of cooking oil. So remarkably unchanging, the inertia of a fast-food cafeteria. But all such things were, of course, the insignificant back-drop, props upon a stage, nothing to do with the real thrill, the star of it all. For there she stood, centre-stage, the only attraction worth sipping your coffee slowly for: Reggie.

'She turns me to jelly you know,' said Bob to Jim Holland. 'There's some erotic kind of power over me, I don't know about you.'

Holland smiled. 'Reggie's played hell with my hormonal balance for years, Bob; I know her well. I used to come here well nigh every evening, and she's always been the biggest cause of my hunger.'

'Yes, it's crazy isn't it? If she had a whip, I'd be in a blissful state of heavenly slavery; perhaps that's why I never stay too long in this place. She's too dangerous to me.'

'In what way, exactly?'

'To my state of mind.'

'Your stability? Are you – Doctor Driscoll, an eminent, honorary consultant – honestly telling me she's got that kind of hold on you?'

'Between you and me, I can't say; don't really know what's happening. Look at it like this. My wife doesn't have any effect; Ralph Johnson, my boss, I couldn't even give a toss about; but her over there, well . . .'

'And there's nobody else?' enquired Holland innocently, looking attentively at Bob's face.

Then in a flash, Bob felt vulnerable as Danny Broughton appeared in three dimensional dynamite in his mind. Reggie was still there, in his vision of desire, but alongside, perhaps almost eclipsed, by a contender of youthful darkness. Bob was in momentary turmoil, those two images which meant so much, had so much power over him: Reggie and Danny side by side, almost locked in a combat, fuelled by Bob's sexual indecision to be able to choose between them. Jim Holland's voice interrupted him, mercifully ending his psychological agony of inability to make a choice. Yet before such an incapacitating turmoil passed, it was maybe Daniel, not Reggie who occupied the greater part of his vision.

'So Rosedale's a garden turned from beautiful to bad, its fruits no longer sweet?' said Holland, proud of his metaphors.

'Downright sour,' grimaced Bob, lighting a cigarette and getting his thoughts into some kind of order. He managed to force himself to concentrate, to get into gear, to give Holland a good picture. He ordered another coffee, blew out smoke and spoke with a serious fluency, using a dialogue removed from any medical jargon, in order to politely put the young reporter at ease, and not feel talked at or down to.

Bob Driscoll finally spoke. 'They're all a bunch of nutter's really.'

'Who?'

'Medics. The whole damn lot of them. Sometimes I seriously question who's the most sane – patients, or those whose job it is to look after them.'

'And are they, do you think, really looked after? Cared for?'

'The sixty-four million dollar question,' said Bob hopelessly, not with any force, just a capitulated, sad and sorry fatalism. He continued, 'It depends really what the ultimate objective is,

the overall goal. You can stabilize somebody who's mentally ill
– or more crucially who has been classed as such – but as to an
outright permanent cure, it's one hell of a muddy river.'

'So which do you side with, which do you favour? The
institution or community care?'

'If it comes to the pinch, as it is going to do, I suppose for
better or worse I'd side with community care – despite all the
fears I hold about its practical aspects and workability. Most
importantly, how this will affect patients emptied out of the
hospital and onto the streets.'

'With one almighty, painful jolt no doubt,' mulled Jim
Holland. 'So then I take it you've tired with, even begun to
loath, the institution, the not-so-rosy Rosedale?'

'It's never been rosy, just an overwhelmingly Philistine camp.
Nowadays a patient doesn't get beaten up and put on a straw
bed with a foot in a ball and chain. Instead a part of the brain
is cut out, or shocked by electricity into moronic submission. It
makes me sick!'

Holland was eagerly writing notes in a rapid, furious
shorthand scribble. 'Which leads me onto something else – this
business of only last week, which a few of my department of
the *Mercury* were involved in . . .'

'Oh, the Drake interview? Yes, a nice publicity stunt for his
ego, for sure. He's a total incompetent, you know! Inadequate,
an amateur butcher. I shouldn't think he'll stay with us much
longer.'

'Why not?'

'Because I for one will do my very best to get him booted out
of Rosedale, and if it really comes to it, kicked out of psychiatry
altogether.'

'It's clear at the very least you and he don't see eye to eye.'

Driscoll took a deep inhalation of cigarette smoke, then
peered deep into Holland's face, his voice cool and controlled,
but firm and precise.

'Look, this Drake scenario could surely be your paper's biggest spring-board since sliced bread. Focus on Drake, read up a bit on your last week's *Mercury* article. Can't you see he's full of crap; dangerous, unprofessional crap? Well?'

'I certainly think from what I know of the guy that he comes over as too good to be true. Pre-rehearsed, smooth, polished speeches, never answering a question incorrectly. I can see your point – he's false. What can you give me on him?'

'All that I've already said – word for word – facts.'

'So it's not a personal thing? A mutual barny?'

'No, not at all – by and large I get along with most of the Rosedale people most of the time. I'd take a good guess and say that Doctor Drake is the only member of Rosedale's entire medical staff that I dislike and feel is inappropriate for such a position. He is irresponsible, unaccountable, and, like I said, bloody dangerous.'

Holland took a gulp of strong coffee. 'Okay, enough for now about Drake. What's all this hornets nest about mis-allocation, maybe misappropriation, of tax payers' money for Rosedale's supposed rehabilitation funds?'

Driscoll sighed, again aware that he needed to have to explain to this reporter things he was so obviously time-worn with. 'It's not embezzlement, there's no financial fraud or monetary skulduggery going on; rather, it's a totally wrong diversion of funds into certain Rosedale departments.'

'For functionaries rather than patients?'

'Patients always ironically come last.'

'Despite official hype to the contrary?'

'Well, we're back to it again, aren't we? Supposed care and concern for our less fortunate brethren being nothing of the sort.'

'There's no real change in quality of patient care?'

'Very little, and what is, is all bullshit; largely an irrelevant, bad co-ordination. A miss-match of scarce resources.'

'Sticking with that, what happened to Rosedale's recent one and a half million quid grant for a patients' rehabilitation update of more recreational, educational facilities and such?'

'Never happened. As I've just told you - patients are last on the Rosedale list.'

'So who are the actual beneficiaries?'

'Let's think, well - a good slice of the cake goes into useless but expensive technical gadgetry to adorn the offices of a cancerous admin sector. Then also a quite hefty bit gets creamed off by the ever-growing swell of managers - appearing at lavish lunches in the sleekest of company cars.'

'Why doesn't it all come to light? Why can't this obnoxious boil burst sometime?'

'It might actually begin to burst fairly soon - Rosedale's not as secret or insulated any more; take as an example our actual chat now.'

Jim nodded, feeling the time was good to explore a nagging, rather personal grievance. 'What's your view on social work - and its personnel?'

'In Rosedale, or just generally?'

'Specifically in Rosedale.'

'A load of balls. A financial drain by lots of much misguided, misinformed, weepy missionaries.'

'Why misguided?'

'They don't approach the actual patients' problems properly.'

'Why misinformed?'

'They don't have a clue as to what even the actual problems are.'

'Why weepy?'

'A sloppy, bearded crew of sociological Florence Nightingales who project their own insecurities and inadequacies onto others, and in doing so, assuage their own self-pity and anxieties. Social work, the pinnacle of the socially superfluous.'

Holland felt boosted, having just had his suspicions about a social work department so well and authoritatively confirmed. Doctor Driscoll – eminent, experienced psychiatrist – had nicely substantiated Jim Holland's growing capacity for hate of the Harrisons of this world. Bob Driscoll had amply confirmed Holland's desired condemnation of Harrison. Whether factual or not, it didn't matter. Jim Holland's axe to grind was given full sway. Jim Holland was beginning to like Doctor Driscoll. For unlike, say, a social worker such as Harrison, Bob Driscoll didn't lie, didn't give any crap.

'Time's getting on,' said Driscoll, glancing at his watch. 'Gill, my wife, will be worrying. Have I given you the sort of stuff you needed, or not?'

Jim Holland stuffed a wad of scribbled-upon, loose notebook pages into his inside jacket pocket. 'You've done me proud,' he said with what seemed a quite sincere face, 'although it might take some time to get the story into shape, into the actual finished piece.'

'That's no problem to me, so long as it's done and is not woolly or weak. I can't stand a willy-nilly pussy-footing article.'

'You won't get that from me,' said Holland. 'I go in hard.'

'Go in hard.'

Both men looked across at the cash counter. Reggie was putting on a maroon leather coat and hat. She'd finished at this café for today; now a drive to another one of maybe several, all part of her ever-expanding fast-food chain.

'It's going to be an empire, you know,' said Driscoll to Holland.

'Without a doubt,' agreed an admiring Jim Holland.

'Her empire,' Driscoll said, as they paid and walked out into the cold evening.

No doubt Jim Holland would be writing, planning the skeleton of a big story under a desk lamp late into the night. He was young and bright, and above all else, ambitious. Quite therefore a totally dissimilar character from Bob Driscoll. For Bob had never been particularly ambitious, certainly never impulsive, and there was never a need to be so for the reason that he could gauge, size up, correctly anticipate changes and opportunities well in time, almost before they arose, and then comfortably react, handle such change accordingly and appropriately. He was a professional, more exactly a strange, rare kind of breed – an entrepreneur of psychiatry with radical but realistic insights brilliantly smuggled in the essential package. The essence of his contribution was a personality badly needed in an age of staid conventionality and immobile bureaucracy. He could cut through red tape with a razor-like inovativeness, could see just that little bit further than most others: an imaginative ingredient in society's boring, bland, plain and tasteless cake.

But it was still even a more complex matter. For whilst a cool, clever external appearance would be seen by those around him as reflecting self-confidence, an unruffled, untroubled demeanour, nothing could be further from the truth. For Doctor Driscoll had a vicious, bitter war going on inside him: his heart versus his brain. As regards his heart, his innermost emotional striving dictated a need to be sincere and loyal to Gill, but his mind told him in no uncertain terms that she was redundant now in his agenda of both present and future. Divorce Gill was the inexorable command and substitute in its place a bisexual recognition, devoid of shame in himself, in his self-image. Such a daunting vision of a crushing self-awareness was a cruel problem, a conflict raging inside him, because if he followed such a procedure through, it would badly hurt Gill, could cost him his career, and most crucially of all, might not necessarily work out anyway in the way he desired. For it had never actually been that Danny Broughton had, on any occasion, touched or kissed Bob Driscoll first.

Bob's mind reeled under such a thought, such a wave of possible truth, that Danny's commitment could be, might always be, lacking. Did Danny, or could Danny – an often mentally disturbed young psychiatric patient – actually reciprocate Bob's love? Incredulously, Bob pondered with grave seriousness upon just such a thing. If that was so, that Danny felt little, even nothing, genuine affection for Bob, then Bob's future would definitely be in total ruin. For he'd lose Gill, his job, and Daniel.

However, poor, sad, tragic victim Gill, his wife for twenty years, would have to be told – sooner rather than later – that he no longer loved her, and that, apart from a provider of ironed shirts for work and an evening meal, she wasn't needed any more. Equally dispensable was Ralph Johnson, the faltering, fumbling, incompetent Rosedale number one. The sooner he left the better, and Bob Driscoll would do all he could to speed that up. Was it perhaps a consistent, subconscious, most powerful drive for the need for Danny Broughton – a drive Bob either didn't genuinely recognise or deliberately made himself blind to – which was responsible for his ruthlessly, almost psychopathically concocted agenda? A list or impersonal format of people to deal with impersonally, manipulate to his own solitary advantage to rescue himself from his growing self-crisis, his possible future disintegration. Was his obsession for Danny the cause of his newly constructed callous resolve? He wondered this, then dismissed such self-introspective guilt with a tenuous reason that all it was really, was a necessary survival tactic, a strategy of no other options or ways in which to approach his present problems or alternative pathways out of his difficult mid-forties crisis of a circumstantial maze.

Bob Driscoll was very tired, bedraggled and brimming almost to a mental over-flow with a thousand worries, imponderables, as he sat with Gill sipping hot strong coffee. He'd done his best to explain his subversion of seeking out Holland and in so doing, maybe through a widespread splash of adverse publicity, dynamite Rosedale hospital. To seal its demise was, Bob said, the only way to break down new productive ground in mental health organisation for the benefit of patients, even if the alternative of community care posed certain problems.

'For first and foremost, Gill,' Bob said, 'the bins, obscene testimonies of man's inhumanity to man, must be shut down, razed to a state of permanent invisibility and as time goes on, an absence of ever having existed.'

Gill spoke. 'Such memories will recede, fade out, Bob, and I'm aware such a project is central to you.'

They lapsed into a thoughtful sad silence and then Gill asked a question which was the really big one, at least for her own information. She asked it quietly but firmly.

'Am I any longer central to you? Do I figure in this tangle still, the thickets you're fighting your way through?'

Bob spoke. 'I'm not sure of anything really right now. To be honest, I just don't know Gill, cannot seem to say. As you say, it's a tangle; it's breaking me up, I feel, at times.'

Bob couldn't find the courage to spit it out; it was so hard to look at his misty-eyed wife and lie. It would have to be said later, shelved for the future. Gill perhaps could easily sense all of this and at that moment of crushing realisation, could have cried an ocean.

But she, instead, squeezed his hand ever so lightly and said with unmistakable truth, 'This tangle you say you're in, I am in too; but whatever the damage or cuts and scars of such thickets that you're in, I'm alongside you all the time, so long as it takes.'

Gill looked at her husband's drawn, worry-etched now sleeping face, kissing it softly. She ascended the stairs quietly, leaving him sleeping on the lounge settee. For some time she sat wistfully upon the edge of the bed feeling a creepingly cold sense of loneliness and heartbreaking premonition that she might already be out on a limb, so terribly alone.

Chapter Ten

Kim Hesketh was careful not to collide with the busy human traffic of a bustling Rosedale corridor. An entire spectrum of different employees raced towards her and, as they got closer, there was a polite manufacturing of smiles of acknowledgement. Whether or not it was a sincere recognition of her well-known efficiency of an experienced ward sister, or a more ulterior motivation of lust for her fantastic face and lovely figure, was debatable. Nonetheless, nobody ignored Kim; she was popular, she was pleasant and she had always put patients first.

For Sister Hesketh was from what could be loosely termed, 'the old school', a bygone nursing age, devoid of managers or other largely superfluous capacities, a time during her training when the essence of psychiatric therapy was of two parties only, patients and ward based nursing staff.

But like it was termed, 'the old school' unfortunately happened to be a relic of a fast-receding occupational altruism, a service of the past. For the 'new school' was, no matter how much its spokes-persons proclaimed to the contrary, an essentially profit making concern. Psychiatric care had insidiously become a business.

Walking towards her, with a couple of files in his arms, as well as a large bunch of papers, was Luke Lloyd Evans, psychologist, medical team member, and long established good friend.

'It's worse than the London or even Tokyo rail underground,

this corridor today,' he joked.

Kim responded with a smile and extended the similes. 'Or a hornets' nest, or a cavern of busy bats!' she said.

'Either way, I'll be very glad to get home tonight. It's been a hell of a week.'

'Hasn't it just!' offered a rather tired Kim. 'What's remaining for you in the winding down hours of a Rosedale Friday?'

'Anything but winding down, I'm afraid. I'm snowed under with work: reports to do, meetings to attend. How about you?'

'Busy as ever.'

'You look a little thoughtful Kim, reflective even. No problems other than the usual?'

'I guess maybe I've been a little bit wistful over recent days, but don't quite know why.'

'Anything to do with the Colin Oakley's of this world? It was on your ward it all happened, if I'm correct?'

'You're right, the same ward, although I was on a day shift.'

'Yes, it was an incident in the middle of the night, wasn't it? Did you have any possible inkling of it actually happening though?'

'No real observational concerns about Colin's behaviour or mood. It didn't seem any different to a usual day as regards Colin. No, but . . .'

'But what?' asked Luke earnestly.

To Luke's question, Kim Hesketh's face betrayed the slightest expression of defensiveness, and she seemed reluctant to reply.

'What is it, Kim? You're holding back on me. What's the matter?'

Still Kim didn't speak, the words frozen upon her lips. Luke sensed possibly why.

'You don't want to drop anybody, or maybe somebody in particular, into hot water; offend someone you think should be answerable for something, yes? Well, it's strictly confidential between us - you know I'd honour that - so what's on your mind about the Oakley incident? Another side of the official story?'

'It might be,' replied a rather reticent Kim, her speed faltering. 'Though I couldn't easily say if it was a direct causal link.'

'Causal link? Causational as to what? Of what? Come on Kim, open up.'

'This isn't the right place to discuss it; too many people milling about. Too many ears,' Kim said. 'We'll find somewhere private, a quiet place. Let's try one of the committee rooms near Reception. I don't think there are any meetings on at this moment.'

Kim and Luke found themselves sitting in a very musty and dusty old room, facing one another over a vast oak table.

'So what is it, then?' asked Luke.

'Well,' said a somewhat guarded Kim, 'I feel not simply sadness, but almost a nagging sense of grievance.'

'As to what exactly, or to whom?'

'It's still very unclear; my reasoning compels me towards a rather suspicious stance, but my professional judgement quells any rash statements by me, any foolhardy impulse.'

'You're saying you're not content to let sleeping dogs lie about the Oakley suicide?'

'Yes, but if I pushed it, that is if I started stirring things up with a view to wanting a different face on the matter, and I was eventually proved wrong, my initial reservations unfounded, then . . .'

'Then you think you'd be dismissed, out on your backside?'

'Exactly. It's a difficult problem and consequently a difficult decision to press my case.'

'Which is . . . ?'

Kim spoke as boldly as her apprehension allowed. 'That I don't think that Doctor Driscoll necessarily failed to prevent the suicide of Colin Oakley at all. At least not as the official view of the case would have it and would allow us to all believe.'

'So, something's afoot? A bit of psychiatric skulduggery, a wrongful condemnation of Bob Driscoll, perhaps? That certain circumstances, due to something quite crucial and as yet unknown to most of us, remains undisclosed?'

'Yes Luke, and not so much undisclosed, but apart from myself, in the entire hospital, still unrevealed. It's not simply fascinating, but a bit eerie; even smacks of the sinister, a dark side of this hospital's rhetoric of a sunny garden.'

'So the reality might be that due to something absolutely crucial, Bob Driscoll's been unfairly, unprofessionally painted with undeserved guilt and incompetence by the likes of Drake and that silly press meeting he was spouting off in.'

'You're getting the picture,' said a now more confident Kim, confident in as much as she felt Luke was not only razor-sharp in powers of incisive thought, but could also be trusted, confided in.'

'It's a bit of a subterfuge isn't it?' he said, lightening their dialogue a bit. 'A conspiracy against our own rank and file? But,' he added, 'it wouldn't be real to assume a medical team consensus, a harmony at all, would it?' He paused, then resumed his central tack. 'What really intrigues me then, from what you've so far said, is just why the anti-depressant pills Bob prescribed didn't work? Why they had no effect upon preventing a nocturnal acute cloud of depression and thereby fail to prevent Colin Oakley's successful consequent self-destruction?'

'That is exactly the point of entry where my opinions start, indeed occupy very dangerous professional ground. I'm walking on thin ice. If I say it openly, it could be construed as diabolical, unprofessional etiquette.'

Luke's voice rose in exasperation. 'Kim, for goodness sake, stand up and be counted! Your opinion's valid, as worthy as that of Ralph Johnson, as valid as anybody's on earth, for that matter. So open up, let your feelings come into the open.' Then hardly a split second later, Luke found himself apologetic. 'Sorry

Kim, I'm sounding like I'm psycho-analysing you, a bit of an academic guru turned bully. Sorry. Take it at your own pace, then maybe after we'll go for coffee.'

'Okay,' Kim said. 'My story, that unheard, unofficial, almost contraband version of it all, goes like this . . .'

Kim then slowly and clearly elaborated upon her worst suspicions. The impression they made upon Luke Lloyd Evans rang agonizing warning bells in his mind. For according to Kim it was not a matter of any anti-depressant tablets failing to work effectively or anything like that at all. The word 'tablets' didn't enter into her version, for the taking of tablets by Colin Oakley was a myth. Tablets were a complete fiction; there had been no tablets of any kind actually administered to Colin Oakley at all.

This was where it began to get very interesting, if disturbingly bizarre. For the only drugs given were not tablets, but a certain medication delivered by injection. There was a world of difference, Kim explained to Luke, between a drug being prescribed, as it in fact was by Doctor Driscoll, and its effective giving or administering. For it was so very true that Bob, hassled and harassed as he was one recent busy morning, did quite rationally and consciously prescribe by word of mouth to a ward nurse that anti-depressant tablets should be given to patient Oakley to try and lift him out of a depressive state. But Bob gave this prescription of medication verbally and not in writing.

But what really was important, what really cut ice, was the issue of whether or not such a consultant's recommendation had actually been put down in writing, in Colin's case notes. In this case, it had not. Doctor Driscoll had not documented it, perhaps feeling that simply informing a nurse of his recommendation for anti-depressant tablets was quite sufficient. Perhaps, as Kim said to Luke, this was an error on Bob Driscoll's part, that he should have actually written it down, to corroborate his verbal decision.

Kim was in full flow now, as Luke listened with deadly seriousness.

'Remember,' she said, 'I told you about the crucial difference between a doctor verbally prescribing a drug and the actual giving of such a drug.'

'Yes,' nodded Luke attentively, 'And . . .'

Kim then said that the important point was not solely the fact that Colin Oakley never actually took, or indeed had been given, anti-depressant tablets. 'That,' said Kim, 'is only the tip of the iceberg in this case. It was what soon followed on my ward which was the decisive factor.'

'Which was?' questioned Luke, who on very rare occasions, as now, lit a cigarette to spur his concentration. He needed to keep a tight bearing upon all of this complex matter, so he brought Kim back to a point she made earlier, which might be relevant to the progression of her argument. 'What then is it about an injection or something you earlier hinted at?'

Kim took off from that point Luke introduced. She explained that Doctor Driscoll, whilst in the midst of discussing Colin Oakley's mental state, and the specific anti-depressant medication appropriate, had been suddenly called to another ward for an urgent matter, and he had not returned to finish his discussion with the nurses about Colin Oakley's medication.

'That,' said Kim, 'left the entire issue open to what was to be a tragic abuse of professional communication, and incorrect medication implementation procedures.'

'In what way was it a communication crisis, if crisis be the correct word?' Luke asked.

'Crisis is highly appropriate, even now in hindsight perhaps an understatement,' Kim added, and continued to explain. 'It was evident that a few hours after Doctor Driscoll's incomplete chat with ward nursing staff about Colin's medication, that a junior registrar named Doctor Winters had happened to be doing a general tour of several wards, including the one housing

Colin Oakley. In particular, Doctor Winters was reviewing medication cards, seeing things were up to date, or that certain dosages of drugs were being adhered to by nursing staff administering them. All in all, Doctor Winters was spending the afternoon in a medication review.

'The upshot was a bit of strange thinking and decision-making by Doctor Winters with nurses, who could not oppose his opinions. In particular, Doctor Winters had focused his attention upon the fact that Colin Oakley, a psychiatric patient, occasionally prone to depressive swings of mood, had currently, and had already had for two years, been on an injection of the anti-psychotic drug, Haloperidol. Doctor Winters felt that in his opinion it would be extremely unwise to prescribe anti-depressants, due to the fact that such tablets would, by nature of their bio-chemical effects, badly clash with the Haloperidol that Colin Oakley was already on. Doctor Winters thus felt that, for Colin Oakley's physical constitution, it would be dangerous in the shape of side-effects for Haloperidol and anti-depressants to be taken together. Doctor Winters told nursing staff that if it had been such a prescription, then severe side effects for Colin could have transpired, ranging from severe muscular cramp to splitting headaches.'

All of this, Kim explained, would not have even taken place if Doctor Driscoll had written up his views of that morning. Since he did not, it gave full rein later in the day to Doctor Winters to overrule him in a way by putting a medical decision in writing. The nature of the prescription effectively determined by Doctor Winters was the most salient aspect of it all. For he not only prevented any administering by ward nurses of anti-depressant tablets, but also decided that some additional drug dosage of some kind was required.

'So what actual drug change did Winters decide upon?' asked Luke, who by now was getting the gist of it all.

'He decided and authorised an increase of Colin's anti-psychotic medicine,' said Kim.

'That actual anti-psychotic medicine being Haloperidol?' said Luke.

'Yes,' Kim replied, 'given by the usual method of injection, and increased by a hundred per cent.'

Luke paused and reasoned his thoughts, for although not being too much up on drug knowledge, he knew enough about general medical matters to understand Kim's account.

He spoke. 'So Winters increased Oakley's injection of anti-psychotic Haloperidol. He doubled it, yes?'

'Yes,' said Kim, now feeling much like either plenty of strong coffee or lots of cool fresh air, anything she thought to get out of the mustiness of the room.

'So then,' said Luke, 'what we have is a situation where Doctor Winters increased Colin Oakley's anti-psychotic dosage, an injection alteration, but not any prescription by Winters of any drug to combat what Driscoll discerned to be Oakley's depressive state?'

'All right so far. But it's still not the full story I've got in my mind, and the climax is the real punch line . . .' Kim gave a relatively jargon-free explanation of often quite severe side effects of psychiatric drugs. 'Because unfortunately,' Kim said, 'although certain of the anti-psychotic medicines can do a lot to stabilize a particular illness, they often also can give some pretty vicious side effects.'

'Such as?' asked Luke, a little bit out of his depth.

'Well, a group of drugs called the phenothiazines, usually for the treatment of schizophrenic disorders, often stabilize the most acute symptoms of an illness quite well. But . . .'

'But what?' enquired Luke.

'. . . But also possess in their actual biochemical molecular chain a rather nasty element – or set of elements – which, if the drug dosage is substantial, can play havoc with a patient's mind and body.'

'Such as making a patient elated one moment, sad the next, or very fatigued, then restless, for instance. Am I right?'

'Yes,' said Kim. 'But what you said about a mood of being sad is especially pertinent here, considering who we're talking about.'

'Colin Oakley's injection of Haloperidol could exert a side effect of feeling low?'

'More than that Luke, far more. It would bring upon – and this is a generally proven side-effect for many patients – a severe bout of depression.'

'I've got the picture now,' said Luke. 'The existing dose of Haloperidol could have been making Colin depressed, and what does Winters do? He bloody well doubles the dose!'

'Exactly. An increase of a drug which has been proved to induce side-effects of depression. Haloperidol is a prime culprit for causing melancholia to those who are given it.'

'And was it a big dose?'

'Quite substantial, yes. And for Doctor Winters to increase it by a hundred per cent seems ludicrous. That action taken could very well have directly precipitated such an acute depressive state of mind and to cause Colin Oakley to commit suicide.'

'Which obviously he did. It's absolutely ludicrous, isn't it Kim? On the one hand Bob Driscoll wishes to alleviate Oakley's depression by prescribing anti-depressant tablets, and yet Winters prescribes exactly the opposite as a subsequent outcome. A bigger dose of the same depressive inducing drug. Then to really put the lid on it, there was Drake's silly press interview, which further distorted and confused things all the more.'

'That's how I personally see things,' added Kim, 'and I don't really want to be quoted, for the simple reason that Colin's suicide, as a consequence of Haloperidol, cannot, I don't think, ever be actually satisfactorily proven.'

'I see your point. It's a difficult one to try and air, especially as you would, or *we* would, get little sympathy or support from lots of other Rosedale medics.'

'They probably wouldn't believe us. Maybe they'd just say it was speculation, a highly tenuous argument to advance at most. So what do we do? Where now?'

'Obviously I'm not psychiatrically versed in drug knowledge, but you've convinced me all the same of a very powerful possibility. What we have is unprofessionalism on two levels. Firstly, Doctor Winters' incompetence; he should never have over-ruled Bob Driscoll albeit indirectly. And secondly, in the capacity of only a junior registrar, which Winters effectively is, he shouldn't be allowed to alter important drug treatments anyway. I'm going to look into that with Ralph.'

'But do you really think Ralph will have an understanding, sympathetic ear?'

'Maybe not. It's highly unlikely he'd take any action against Winters, but I can still make pretty damn certain that Ralph knows our side of the story.'

'I said I'd prefer not to be quoted, Luke.'

Luke, once again, felt his irritation levels rising. 'Here we go again,' he said, raising his voice to Kim. 'Just when will you ever stand up and make your own views or grievances known? When in fact, will most of our Rosedale phantoms, for that matter?'

'Phantoms?' said Kim.

'Yes,' said Luke. 'People who always prefer a place in the shade don't have enough vigour or confidence in themselves to hardly ever take a stand.'

'But Luke, I did say it was only a hypothesis of mine, that it couldn't necessarily be proved. Having said that, I could really drop myself in it if you spouted such an unprovable set of opinions I have. Can you see my side of it? My situation?'

Luke blew out a confused sigh then rubbed his eyes. 'Yes, Kim, I suppose you're right, and again I've been too abrasive with you. I'm sorry, and I mean that. Maybe I'll still air the view you have to Ralph, but not quote you, not mention any names. I'll play it very carefully.'

'I hope so,' sighed an equally weary, worn and torn Sister Hesketh.

'I think it's definitely set a precedent,' commented Ralph Johnson, 'this discussion about a dead patient.'

'Almost bizarre,' added Luke Lloyd Evans, 'especially when it's about strictly clinical matters.'

'So we're here to broach some issues, even if no dramatic conclusions are found?' stated Ralph.

It was almost as if Ralph was bored to even discuss the tragedy, instead simply hoping it would all blow over, be kept under raps, not hit the press. Such an attitude emanated from what he was saying. 'You see, no matter how upsetting this incident must be for a lot of us, the nature of a psychiatric hospital does have such unpredictable events inevitably built into it.'

'You're saying, then,' said Trish Turner, 'that we must coolly and calmly expect the occasional suicide, possible incompetence of psychiatrists, and just say to a dead patient's grieving relatives, that of course it's a sorry thing to have to happen, but life's tough?'

Ralph immediately reacted to Trish Turner's dry sarcasm. 'That's unfair, uncalled for, and totally out of professional order, Trish!'

An insightful Luke chipped in. 'But Ralph, what can be more utterly unprofessional than one massive "balls-up" like this? We are looking at a flesh-and-blood issue, not a balance sheet or a nosy media waiting in the wings. We're talking about something completely atrocious insofar as it reflects any notions of your admiration for our ostensible professionalism.'

Ralph countered him. 'Actual facts of this incident apart, because there's still no complete explanation, just what do you expect us to do, us sitting here right now? All burst into a flood of tears? Pack in our jobs here and look for a career which never includes anxiety or trauma for its practitioners, people like ourselves.' He continued to speak despite Luke's attempts to interrupt. 'So should we all now jointly hand in our notice, resign from Rosedale on the grounds of having mistakenly taken it upon ourselves to do too emotionally demanding a job? Well? *What* I ask you.'

Ralph would never reason. Trish and the other members present saw in Ralph a sad, sorry, broken man, one who would be more useful to society and its people if he simply quit his post and opened up a grocery business.

Trish Turner broke the strained silence. She saw very little point in continuing the meeting. 'I guess it's been a bloody awful day for all of us, all parties concerned. Not least Colin Oakley's shattered relatives. Ralph, do you suggest I see them now, try and offer something useful?'

'Yes, placate and console such victims of tragic circumstance. I feel you are the one for that, Trish.'

The meeting broke up and ten minutes later Colin Oakley's solicitor and next of kin were asking Trish Turner some very tough questions.

Chapter Eleven

Ralph Johnson had been dreading it. Since faxed to him directly over three months ago, it all hung over him like a brooding, morose thunderstorm. At any moment he could be caught by the lightning flash of change, and Ralph, set and staid in his ways, didn't like change. Yet it would be both unfair and incorrect to say he was fossilised into a rut of inaction. Ralph could adapt, was alert, could be flexible in what was a recently rapidly changing system: a fundamental transformation of the system of mental health. So, yes – he could adapt. But what he couldn't seem to be able to do was be decisive. His lack of any firm conviction was his biggest flaw, a huge fault in any medical director. With an important meeting in just under an hour, no wonder Ralph was apprehensive, even frightened.

Everybody in Rosedale knew that Ralph had not always been a 'yes' man of bureaucratic inaction. Only over the last couple of organisationally complicated, confusing years in Rosedale had his irritating inertia set in. And to be fair to him, it might well not be his fault, but instead, that of a bureaucratically suffocating circumstance, pertinent to the vastly complex closing years of the twentieth century. An age whereby modern organisational shackles for a medical director are not simply obligatory, but stifling and compulsory. He, individually, might not actually be to blame – nor indeed might Bob Driscoll – but instead, the cruel culprit of unpredictable circumstance. For after all, if human beings are not perfect, then it could no doubt logically follow that their ideas, plans, and ambitions revealed in the institutions they build are also doomed to inevitable flaws of imperfection. To expect anyone in difficult contemporary times to be superman or superwoman would be a totally unreasonable stance, an illogical, irrational one. Above all, it would be an expectation of an unrealistic mind, and hence, perhaps, one skirting around a border of diminished powers of reason.

Such wisdoms of rare intellect were at full play inside Ralph's head as the clock showed it was time to attend a conference of which Ralph could easily, in advance, predict its likely and largely useless outcome. A meeting which would be a waste of time. And as Ralph had predicted so succinctly, so assuredly, the morning had turned out to be a farce.

A couple of Treasury accountants, a Home Office representative, a Health Department official and some of Rosedale's administrative cream had foraged around in the dark without signposts or beacons to guide them towards any conclusions. A 'talks about talks' discussion devoid of anything original, anything refreshingly new.

The meeting had begun with a severe message from the Health Service Minister about an inevitable descending financial axe, wielded by the financial 'bods' of Westminster. The ultimatum was being softly and indirectly given, a deliverance of a command that entailed a pruning of cash for Rosedale, a cutback in resources. The really critical question of exactly upon whom in Rosedale the Exchequer's axe would most mercilessly fall was irritatingly couched in evasive terms.

Ralph could so well have anticipated such an outcome. In fact, at one point in the meeting, he was very tempted to cut through all the thickets of dry diversionary language and ask that crucial question: just who in Rosedale would actually be hit the hardest. But he decided not to ask; his silence being for two good reasons. First of all, the Minister would not commit himself to being forthcoming, open about specifics, about details of cut-backs and the resulting victims. This, in Ralph's long experience, was always the case. But secondly, and much more importantly, the reason Ralph didn't ask what would seem possibly the most important question of all – that of who was to suffer from financial pruning – was that because Ralph already knew the answer. It would, as it had always been, a cutting back of resources which would affect patients – the actual clientèle of Rosedale would feel the harsh brunt of it all. For Ralph knew that a cost-conscious Government, of any political slant, always looked and preyed upon the most vulnerable victims, those who couldn't muster up much opposition. So psychiatric patients, powerless, lacking in political clout and credibility in the eyes of society, and possessing very little resources and organisation, would be those first in line to suffer. This was always so, without exception.

So, thought a slightly disillusioned medical director during his lunch hour, what was the point of even mooting such a question. That was the overpowering, the crowing glory of it all, in the psychiatric system. You could quite easily put forward excellent arguments – cutting, insightful points of view on a highly professional basis – but whether or not anything actually got done about your concerns or proposals was a totally different matter altogether.

Suddenly his wry contemplation was broken by a soft tapping upon the door. It was Suzy White. Ralph pointed to one of the plush leather chairs which Suzy not only appeared to sink in, but almost shrink in. Neither of them spoke straight away. Each, without any strain, looked at one another's face.

Ralph broke the silence. 'The meeting was, well, guess?'

'I can't guess,' Suzy replied.

'Crap, bilge, sloppy, word-mongering, a game of amateur spoken Scrabble. Quite frankly, it would have been more productive for me if I'd gone to sleep for an hour.'

'But instead you had to sit it out.'

'Regrettably, painfully, yes. And, talking about pain, or let's say discomfort of a physical kind, that's a reason to now talk. Anybody here knows what I'm about to divulge.'

Suzy poured a glass of water and slowly got around to lighting a menthol cigarette.

'That's the kind of thing connected with what I've got to say, about my health, although I rarely smoke, and the diet and weight's okay – I'm in a pretty bad way,' Ralph said.

'I know you've seen a whole string of GPs because of what you've openly told me: gone to appointments, left me to "man" the ship. But, is there then something I don't know yet? The way you're talking I certainly suspect there is.'

'Yes, true,' Ralph continued. 'I'll throw a question at you. How do you fancy the post I'm soon to effectively quit, or abandon? Or maybe the word is forsake?'

'Are you coming clean, or is it a mid-morning test of my psychological functioning?' Suzy said cautiously, but without inhibitions.

'Straight up, Suzy, no kidding, I'm knackered. That is, I think, the vogue word these days to describe how I feel. I'm on my way out as regards good health and also on my way out of this place.'

'So you're serious, Ralph; no jest, no hidden meanings?'

'Absolutely honest, Suzy. You see, I've finally decided upon it. I'm beguiled by visions of early retirement. A state of mind no longer sitting in this office talking into two phones at once or having to attend kindergarten parties which masquerade as meetings like the one just an hour ago.'

'Well, no doubt after I've been in that chair of yours for ten years, I too will feel the same.'

'What, knackered?'

'Yes Ralph, knackered, but still keen to take on such a post all the same.'

Ralph momentarily studied Suzy's face. Was she a little too ambitious, he wondered, too career conscious? Was she lonely outside the protective Rosedale walls? Was her professional career a cocoon, one that contained all work, no play? Ralph felt a little bit awkward all of a sudden as he contemplated such notions in her presence. About this particular matter of his replacement there was not much more to elaborate upon, to be said. He looked at her heavily powdered face and lilac lipstick while her wisps of cigarette smoke reached the shallow ceiling.

'There's lots of things to say, Suzy, but as regards the job, you can have it,' he said quite calmly. At that exact moment when he announced it to her, he studied her reaction, especially in her eyes. He almost felt uneasy for a split second as a glint of triumph seemed to show through her usually glazed, unrevealing eyes.

Often Ralph pondered as to whether she was very lonely, maybe her efficient career was a disguise for an insufficient life of fun. Possibly she had, at some earlier time, been badly, emotionally hurt: once bitten, twice shy. Ralph devoted lots of time to character studies of his colleagues and although Bob Driscoll, Luke Lloyd Evans and Doctor Drake were quite dark horses, puzzles of somewhat elusive personality profiles, they were not a patch upon Suzy. She was so impenetrable and it seemed would like no doubt to remain so. For Ralph could never quite bring himself to ask about her private life, for such a question was bound to either anger her greatly, or simply allow her to put up yet more barriers and screens to shield herself in what could be called her psychological dark room. For just as a solitary photographer needs lots of time in the dark to do his work to develop films, Suzy needed such a darkness as a defence from intrusion; but just why she did, Ralph never got to find out.

Chapter Twelve

The same old story. Once again it directly reflected a cost-cutting drive. Teenagers, hassled, hot and bothered, flying around the smelly Rosedale staff canteen. Duncan Moon, Divisional Nursing Manager and his lunchtime companion Suzy White, peered through the thick smoky haze.

Duncan Moon guiltily decided to contribute to the heavy, stale atmosphere as he lit a small cigar. *It never used to be like this* he kept thinking, his nostalgic waves breaking upon his disillusioned shoreline of the contemporary shambles that regrettably Rosedale hospital had become.

There was scarcely a vacant chair available. Around the tea-stained tables was a myriad of different kinds of employees. Eager, if rather naive, gormless-looking students who spent roughly six weeks upon a particular ward before being sent to train upon another, all reflected Rosedale's expensive and superfluous expansion of yet more and more personnel upon the pay-roll. It was a bloated creature which could no longer prevent its own swelling, blindly sucking in more mass, getting more and more grotesquely bloated. It was a cancerous growth, out of control. Duncan Moon knew this sad fact only too frighteningly well as he gazed with dismay and listened to the buzz of break-time conversations.

Duncan had heard it all before, *ad nauseam*. He looked at a group of consultants, sombre, in suits, sipping coffee, using their arms and hands a lot to express their particular argument.

No doubt they were talking about a proposed new suite of air-conditioned offices, or the proposal for a staff leisure complex, to be an annex of Rosedale. Either way, essentially mid-morning trivia, a confused clatter of trivial chatter to fill in those minutes between ten and ten-thirty.

'Anyway, congratulations,' said Moon to Suzy, as she added some sweeteners to her coffee. 'You must be feeling well, how should I say . . .'

'Over the moon?' Suzy smiled, her pun borrowing his surname, as they relaxed, leaning back into rather uncomfortable wooden chairs. 'There's lots I'd like to do to this place,' she said with some rigour in her voice.

'But *can* you?' questioned Moon. 'There are no doubts about your capability, but rather I'm thinking of what I might refer to as "notorious Rosedale constraints".'

'Constraints. In what capacity, exactly?' asked Suzy, meeting his thoughtful, experienced eyes.

'From a faceless, but mighty bunch, who walk the Whitehall corridors of power. The ones we only hear from, never see.'

Duncan studied her secretive face. It never, or only very rarely, betrayed an emotion other than an expression indicating business-like grandeur, but whether that could be rightly classed as an emotion was debatable. Duncan decided a strategic change of conversational tack might help, a useful departure from official, work-stultifying talk.

He lit another little cigar, blowing out cool, blue wisps of smoke and spoke. 'Bob, our main medical man, is not having it too easy of late, is he? What's your view?'

'I don't often cross paths with him much these days, far less, in fact, than when I first started.'

'Which was, let's think, ten years ago?'

'Twelve altogether; twelve years nine months. I was just thinking of that earlier on today,' Suzy rather wistfully added.

'You said that with a touch of the old heart strings Suzy,'

added Duncan interestingly.

'More melancholic really,' Suzy said, looking across the room into space and with what appeared, reminiscence in her gaze.

'And do I take it that there's some, if only slight, link with Bob in your reflective harking back through time, or am I just too damn nosey? Tell me please if I am, then I'll wrap up. Well . . .'

'No, don't wrap up, don't silence this topic. It's a thing you might be able to assist me with.'

'A problem?'

'Of sorts.'

'But I take it, certainly no full-blown crisis? No private life catastrophe?'

'No, at least not yet.'

'You mean it could develop into a crisis then?'

'With your help, hopefully not, that's why I need some general information as regards Bob.'

Duncan Moon felt a little perplexed. He thought Suzy's approach to such a topic was like a formal, emotionally antiseptic format of a meeting. Information. That word, and Suzy's use of it, as regards a close colleague; it was as if Suzy White was officially requiring and requesting a computer run-down on a potential business opportunity. Bob's extrinsic worth. An asset. That being so, and Duncan Moon feeling just that impression, decided to proceed carefully but with a little bit of psychology. For he, at that exact moment, had the advantage over Suzy on this matter, because he wasn't quite as ignorant, uninformed or unacquainted as she was. For once, Duncan was in the driving seat, in control in Suzy's presence. Duncan's toes wriggled as he found such a coffee break no longer boringly routine; instead, it was becoming a little exciting.

He chose his point of entry. 'Have you ever thought that Bob's life, and how he lives it, may fairly closely mirror your own? An unconscious reflection, but a real tragedy, despite that.'

113

'Tragedy?'

'In as much as two lonely lighthouses get battered by the same waves of the same sea. But the cruelty of it is, that the lighthouses are at opposite ends of the ocean, never seeing, meeting, aware of one another.'

Suzy wondered. She certainly stood in a hell of a raging sea, smashed with waves, and of that she was chronically aware. But Bob? Was Duncan hinting at something she'd never contemplated – or believed credible – that Bob was in such a pounding torrent too? No, Suzy couldn't accept that, no way. He had Gill, a marriage now into its twentieth year, and a glorious pay-packet of a profession. No, Bob couldn't be lonely, at least, not like her. Suzy saw only herself as estranged, and yet why was Duncan Moon talking like this? Just what was going on?

'Is this a bit of a joke, Duncan, or what?' she countered.

'No laughing matter at all. No,' Duncan replied with serious lines in his face. 'In fact, it's all so terribly real.'

'Then how do you account for his twenty year bond with Gill?'

Duncan lowered his voice. 'Bob doesn't love Gill any more; she's not the same woman that he once, all too lovingly, married.'

'I don't understand. He seems so full of things to do, people to see, appointments to attend.'

'That's business, nothing to do with what we are touching on, Suzy. Bob Driscoll's Rosedale schedule is just, and only, a Rosedale schedule. Nothing to do with Gill or life outside these four walls.'

He posed another question. 'Would your interest be a sign of *just* interest or more?' Duncan had known Suzy a long time, it wouldn't be too personal an affront for him to ask such seemingly sensitive questions. However, with most others it would be an intrusion and Suzy would angrily react, yet of course not so with Duncan Moon.

He continued, tapping his cigar ash into a large, heavy glass tray. 'I suppose it's a mutually perceived need, something I don't even have to tell you; you know yourself better than me, but maybe I can let you into something you don't know, may find incredible, shocking or just plain bloody morally repugnant, a fact you'd love to imagine otherwise.'

'What is it? What's going to shock me?'

'Maybe not so much shock, as strangely surprising . . .'

'Come on, no fencing, quit word games. What?'

Duncan met Suzy's eyes. 'Did you ever discern Bob Driscoll's inclination to both sexes?'

Rather than frown, or be taken aback, or violently grimace, Suzy threw her head back in a very rare, sudden burst of laughter. 'You're joking, of course,' she said, but then the smile froze and disappeared. 'But you're not, are you?'

'No, I'm not. Bob has a marriage, which to him is now well-nigh meaningless, although Gill still loves him, supports him all the way through the storm he's trying hard to ride at present.'

'What's there for him to overcome? I sense always he's in control.'

'He's not in control Suzy, he's desperately out of control. His sexual conflicts dictate his sorrow, a sorrow he can't alter.'

'He loves another man?' Suzy said, mouth agape at this revelation of astonishing truth.'

Duncan did not answer that particular question, despite his awareness of Danny's power over Bob. Some things, Duncan thought, are personal secrets.

'All I can say is that Bob's unhappy, physically run down and in a difficult position. Actually, I don't know for sure if Gill knows about all this.'

'But if she did?'

'Then I feel she'd still keep on loving him. That's Gill, you see.'

Duncan sensed the rather heavy atmosphere which was

115

developing and glanced at his watch. 'Break over,' he said to Suzy, who had smoked over three cigarettes in half an hour.

'You know,' said Duncan, 'why don't you phone Bob and have a good chat, iron out a few unknowns? Share your mutual concerns. I think Bob could do with a bit of your company, your time, and I think you'd feel better too.'

Suzy stubbed out her cigarette and stood up to go back to her office. 'Yes,' she added, 'it would be nice to talk. I'll phone him.'

The need to talk. Word exchanges, never so badly needed as now, between casualties of the modern age. A paradox: never before was there so much knowledge, information, communication as now, yet never such a desperation, a loneliness, a need to be recognised and so dearly loved as now.

Just two such casualties of the war of harsh circumstances, in an unhappy age, sat together over a late meal in Suzy White's apartment. Bob poured the coffee and Suzy thoughtfully watched the cups fill with the black liquid. As a preliminary, they'd both been merely breaking the ice of recent lack of familiarity, this done by way of chatting about work, such things as Health Service policy and the overhanging cloud of community care. All such changes, they agreed, quite powerfully having a bearing upon their own careers and livelihoods. Stimulating semi-intellectualism, but what they both eventually got round to broaching were the really 'nitty gritty' issues of great concern to them both, as it all so heavily affected them both.

Bob spoke freely, maybe his outgoing frankness and lack of reticence being bolstered by quite a few glasses of red wine. Suzy was more guarded, a little bit reluctant to divulge at first, but after gaining a feeling of mutual confidence, began to open up.

As yet, Suzy had not married, nor at the moment did she

have a lover, her past being a turbulent time of diploma swotting, and all sorts of interviews for successive promotions. Never once had she put a foot wrong on the ladder.

But such a tunnel vision, such an arduous climb, had its price. A missing out on other things, exactly those things that now she craved. And indeed it was a craving, an addiction to warm masculine ruggedness, a desire to be touched, ever-so-sensitively kissed, breathed upon. Of all men she had ever seen or spoken to, Bob Driscoll came perhaps top of the list. Suzy liked him a lot. But whether what she felt for him was a thing called love, she didn't know, couldn't be sure, for she had so little experience of sensations which might have given her better powers of judgement and discretion. Suzy had learned and studied at college after college, but she had lived so little. If you'd told her that fact just five, or even three years ago, she would have scoffed with mocking scorn, an arrogance of your supposed ignorance of her haughty pride of academic superiority.

Suzy White used always to be, Bob thought, as he sat in her lounge, a very difficult person to get on with. But not now. She'd mellowed into a sad, but rather restless situation, almost bordering on a mentally impulsive panic, a salvage operation, before her season of ripeness was over, giving way to wastes of perpetual winter.

As far as Suzy was concerned, Gill didn't matter; she wasn't now in Suzy's game, had been already ousted, just a flimsy insignificant ghost who had been exorcised as part of the rules of the game. Suzy's game. Suzy made the game, the rules, the state of play, crucially of who would play and who would not, and she would always, *must* always win.

Bob was in a way sensing such things himself as regards her line of conversation. At one point she'd seized upon his innocent comment of Gill being away, down south for a couple of days, at her mother's, and suggested to Bob he was very welcome to spend the entire evening and night. Bob had not found that too easy to decline, not for any reasons of lust or guilt of betraying Gill, but quite simply his difficulty in letting Suzy accept a polite 'no' for an answer.

As far as Suzy White was concerned, what she desired she must have, what she wanted was the most important demand in the universe. Already she was of the opinion Bob would agree, for it was not just any woman who desired him, it was instead someone special: it was Suzy White.

Chapter Thirteen

Prisons of passion. The prison of unfeeling, unsympathetic circumstance, a fortress oblivious to the heartbroken cries of its captives, so hopelessly confined within. Bob Driscoll and Suzy White were just two such captives, locked up for their crimes of indecision – despite such transgressions not deliberately of their own making.

But from within, Bob had an accompanying apprehension that he may no longer be reasonably comfortable having a bisexual inclination, having instead a worrying homosexuality. For he didn't love Gill any more, nor Suzy White; no women at all. Even Reggie Carrero was only in his admiration for her business panache and female occupational triumph. That only; he didn't actually feel a loving for her; he also knew full well that she didn't love him. But he felt a driving direct line of passion so hot, so sultry for a young man with jet black hair, very white skin, who happened to be a psychiatric client on his caseload. It was exactly that crushing feeling of powerlessness which made almost everything he wished to alter seemingly unchangeable. That key and the hard quest for it. Whilst still searching for such a method of escape from emotional imprisonment, the key was taunting; it was fate having a field day, enjoying itself as its victims, such as Bob or Suzy, wallowed, injured, helplessly in the mud. The essence of the key which had the power to unlock all inhibitions, set free all those confined and end the darkness of the dungeon was of a gift of unproblematic love.

Bob Driscoll had to delve very deeply into so much of his inner reserves of strength and optimism, even though such reserves were well-nigh empty, run dry. He was in a horrible struggle with his conscience – the bad way he was treating Gill, the dilemma of needing to confide, but also of practical commonsense to withhold. The divulging of all he'd so far done would almost certainly spell not only his material ruin, but destroy the stability of his own mental wellbeing, his constitution.

All such forebodings crystallized in Bob phoning an ex-directory number of a place only he knew about and visited. It had been going on for six months; what might at first appear to be the ultimate paradox of humiliation. Certainly, as he rolled up in his Jag, creeping along a narrow suburban avenue, close on ten o'clock at night, Bob too, felt such humility: for an eminent psychiatrist, qualified as Bob was so widely acknowledged to be, actually seeking out help from another similarly skilled practitioner. This was no ordinary secret, but a super secret; this above all else must always remain solely the knowledge of only two people on earth: Bob and Doctor Maunders.

As he sipped a glass of water, Doctor Maunders took a deep breath in an attempt to stop hiccups which he'd been annoyingly plagued with since his six o'clock rushed meal. He'd already seen seven clients throughout the day, all for an hour's session.

'What is it then about female genitalia that you recently find so repugnant?'

'Not so much repugnant,' said Bob rather sleepily from his slumped position in a chair, 'rather it doesn't seem to mean as much lately.'

'You're saying you have outgrown standard, hot-blooded, heterosexual directions. That it's all played out, boring? You therefore mean, your latest escapism is masculine fantasy, a reflection of your own anatomy?'

'I don't love myself.'

'How can you be so sure, Bob? Can you actually prove to me that your own sexual gratification is not the most important desire which you at present possess and wish to fiercely protect, preserve and give a full flourish of ecstasy? Convince me you're not currently narcissistic.'

'I don't, of late, love myself one little bit; in fact I'm hating myself more each and every minute of the day.'

'Yes, but don't you see my point? You may hate your job, your work colleagues and how you dismally try to cope and muddle through. Yes, I can buy that, but that's not the point I'm making to you.'

'What then? What are you driving at?'

'I'm driving right at the middle of your crisis, its origin, and its self-perpetuating engine, which I can now diagnose. You want to hear it?'

'Yes, tell me, even if it predisposes me to yet more of the same bloody misery I live in, as my mid-forties purgatory.'

'Right, it's unconventional, unusual. Whereas most guy's not far from clocking up an age of fifty have a mid-life crisis, a difficult transition, you don't.'

'What do you assume I have then?'

'Not a *life* crisis, but a *love* crisis.'

'Most of us have love wrangles, hassles, heart-breaks, though . . .'

'Yes, but not many of us have your distinctive – how shall I phrase it? – philosophical style of love. You're always chasing your own tail, looking for more and more, when there is not necessarily any more available.'

'You're saying I'm trying too hard?'

'No, I'm not saying that at all. I'm saying you look at sex and love through a totally different lens than most, and that lens is an analytical one; you're too analytic, you're thinking when you should be ejaculating.'

'I don't see what you're trying to pin point precisely.'

Doctor Maunders sat back in his deep comfortable chair, still playing with his beard. 'Okay, let's try a different angle, a different way of looking at this. What is love? Try and define it.'

'An unselfish, unconditional relationship. A total devotion.'

'You really think so? I've two things to say to that. First, you're talking absolute crap, and secondly, you've fallen completely into the trap I set for you.'

'Well, I'll now ask you for two answers to what you've just said. Okay?'

'Okay, fire away.'

'First of all, why do you say my definition of love is crap, when I thought it sincere and accurate? And secondly, what's the trap you set, the snare that you tell me I've fallen into?'

'I can answer both your questions in one. Your definition of love is crap because of the actual reason why you fell into the trap: you're far too analytic. You tried to specifically formulate a definition of something undefinable. Also your way of approaching, arriving at that definition was robotic; you're far too mechanical. You try to analyse emotions in a logical way. You try to be formally objective in responding to subjectivity.'

'You're saying I'm quantifying things I shouldn't.'

'Yes, you're suffering from too much career-induced analysis; thinking when you should be unhesitatingly feeling. You plan love, all of it down to the last detail. Stop treating your sex life, love life, as an occupation. Love isn't a factory you have to slave away in, you just feel your way, not work yourself into some neurosis.'

Bob opened his eyes slowly. 'So you're simply saying I need to relax, loosen up, not be so intense?'

'Not quite that, no. Just try each day to jettison your philosophy. For love can't, as you seem to think, be studied, rationalised. Okay?'

Bob sighed. 'Okay, and I guess that's my hour nearly up.'

'Just about, yes. No doubt you'll give some consideration to what we've just been talking about, in order to actually use the insights we've arrived at?'

'Yes,' said Bob, sipping water from what seemed a rather dirty glass. He paid cash, all two hundred in twenties, put on his coat and said goodbye to Maunders. But Doctor Maunders was no longer listening, for their hour of talk was over, and Doctor Maunders was busy. He had yet another client to see.

Suzy White knew. She was aware of Bob's underground visitations to a counsellor. In fact she was a little bit annoyed. Her irritation stemmed from her rugged, professional idol having to see a Doctor Maunders; being unable to satisfactorily resolve any problems himself. Suzy couldn't understand why someone as learned and experienced in the science of the human mind should lack the ability to easily solve any problems that he might confront, any hassles coming his way.

Another way of describing Suzy's reaction to Bob's sessions with Maunders was that he went down in her estimation as regards her hitherto opinion of Bob's intelligence and ability. That was why, in a subtle way, she was niggled about it. She wanted to believe Bob was all she admiringly thought, and what she credited to him in her complimentary evaluation. Her dream of Bob's high mental ability was thus flawed somewhat by such a relation of his dependency of having to seek help from Maunders rather than satisfactorily handle any of his own difficulties himself – as she thought Bob always could and would. It made her annoyed that Bob wasn't living up to her image of him as superman; not so elevated, talented or special, as her inflexible construct of him required. When her perfect picture of him ever became a little bit tainted, it caused her annoyance; his real world actions and thoughts interfered with her idealism.

His fallible reality clashed with all her unrealistic expectations. Such a disappointment only made Suzy White's perfectionist personality clearer still. Nothing about any of her fellow human beings should ever go wrong, underperform, let her down. Her practical working definition of others was a direct application of formal Rosedale administrative principles.

Thus appeared Suzy White's quite serious cracks in what so many thought was a smooth professional slate, a confident capable demeanour. For those cracks, or more accurately schisms in her character, were undoubtedly pathological. Her image in reality was nicely summed up in a diagnosis of an egoistical paranoia of neurotic self-protectionism. The coping skills she used to get her through the day, deal with other people, were maladaptive, also unbalanced, as regards social acceptability. This mental state had justification itself for Suzy by erasing any self-perceived contradictions by way of her self-deception and projecting all of her inadequacies onto others. People who she kidded into being her friends ironically got the full blast of her wrath which was generated by her failings, her social unsuccessfulness. But for one person in particular it was terribly worse: Bob Driscoll. He was the only person alive whom Suzy White felt attached to, would openly admit to feeling any love for – even though such love didn't really exist. Suzy White in reality only loved Suzy White. The reason for it being different from more usual love rifts and tangles was that if Suzy was denied what she desired, she could be extremely dangerous; she could not tolerate denial.

It was a hell of a problem, for Bob had confided the gist of his talks with Jim Holland, and the motives, over their recent dinner at her place. She knew about his sessions with Maunders and also quite a bit about his bisexual inclination, which additionally was something she just couldn't accept: a love for another man, a psychiatric schizophrenic patient under Bob's care. All such items of knowledge were quite juicy gems for a bloody good attempt by Suzy at blackmail, if she so wished; the blackmail of Bob Driscoll, if he declined to love her.

Should he choose to not reciprocate her desires, as he knew was in fact the case, he would be a prime candidate for the wrath of hell, all due to a powerful woman's scorn. It was agony to even contemplate the outcome, how it all might come to an ugly unpleasant conclusion. The end might be his career as a psychiatrist; over forever, a bitter divorce from Gill, and publicity, via the media, over that and the hyped-up press sensationalistic saga of his seedy relationship with one of his own male patients. But above all, a betrayal widely publicised to all his kind, all his Rosedale colleagues as a result of his encounters with Holland.

There was no easy way out of what, for anyone, was a crippling dilemma – one without any real options. It was totally impossible, Bob felt, to try and persuade Suzy otherwise; no way would she budge, her sights were firmly and stubbornly fixed and unalterable. But that was only half the reason for the splitting headaches Bob had. The other half of all this agony which he so unfairly seemed to bear entirely on his own was that Suzy's potential items to blackmail him if she wished, were of a nature if used, of a substance, which couldn't be worse in the implications for Bob. Suzy, in a crazy irrational way, said she loved Bob, but simultaneously said to him that she hated him, due to the actual things he'd recently done – the specific things she could blackmail him on. It was no ordinary potential blackmail – whereby knowledge is a damaging weapon to use – but a situation in which the agent had a crusade against the kind of behaviour which constituted such blackmail material. Suzy lived for Rosedale, for her it must never be shut down due to any adverse publicity; equally, Suzy couldn't with her moralistic principles, comprehend homosexuality between a doctor and his patient.

Chapter Fourteen

Some people call it fate, others simply refer to it as change. Unexpected occurrences which, much to human surprise, can put a totally new and different gloss onto a previously familiar, seemingly unalterable picture. Out of the blue, some twist or turn of sweeping unanticipated development, ramifying through former habituated patterns of lifestyles, hopes, fears. In Rosedale hospital, a centre of forensic psychiatry, although virtually almost all personnel were aware of the future scenario of the hospital slowly being run down - its function being transferred to the community - nobody would have expected the suddenness of such an institutional closure as was announced by letter and by briefings one mid-week morning. Such a directive from the very top of the Health Service was of the nature of a complete closure of Rosedale in approximately, but no later than, the next twelve months.

The potential repercussions for all those employed within Rosedale were staggering. New posts would have to be sought out and applied for in the open community setting. All those jobs, which for so long had been so complacently seen as secure and guaranteed within the mental institution, now gave way to a paranoid uneasiness of occupational swirling flux. Future jobs may not be at all easy to find, may not even be available; previous skills acquired through training within the institution may now be rendered obsolete. Such an unsettling state of mind was but one of many offshoots of unwelcome change, something that many Rosedale staff found to their distaste, and was a development which was badly planned and hastily announced. Too much seemed to be happening too fast and too soon.

But for Doctor Driscoll it was not such an unwelcome panorama at all – in fact, it resonated nicely with his long-held, deeply-wished desires; it was all so very well in tune with a great deal of his, what could be called, philosophy of the matter of psychiatric treatment: how it should occur, by whom, and where.

Although Bob had many misgivings about patients turfed out onto the cold community streets of a possible unwelcoming, even hostile public, he nonetheless preferred such an option – one that now to his pleasure was happening. The notion of institutional decarceration was now effective, official Government policy. No more Drakes electrically shocking patients in secret asylum clinics, no more tragic undetected attempts at suicide in lonely patient bedrooms on understaffed wards, no more of all the out of date philistinism that the asylum stood for and had in a sinister, covert fashion concealed for so terribly, tragically long. But also, as far as Bob Driscoll was concerned, with what could be said his 'public' life, there were now some very beneficial changes in his private life as a consequence of the boon of Rosedale's closure.

Widespread change with its shake-ups meant that Suzy's possible tactic of what could be called blackmail of the Driscoll-Holland liaison, was now significantly defused of its potency. It was a small, even petty bomb, incapable of a blast to warrant Bob Driscoll much concern. For if Rosedale had remained a viable concern with a survival into the future, then Suzy would have truly had Bob like a helpless fly in a web; the dire implication of Bob attempting a Rosedale sabotage with a target of its closure via adverse publicity would have maybe landed Bob in jail. That was no exaggeration of the seriousness of his dealings with the popular press. Now that the intended closure was both officially confirmed and to occur within a matter of months, such a transformation altered the antagonistic nature of Bob and Suzy's relationship. In a nutshell, Suzy's power of antagonism was considerably reduced, for with all sorts of Rosedale job changes and eventually the bulldozers razing it totally to the ground, Bob's act of breach of confidence was no longer in any way as serious. Who really cared now so much about Bob's intended exposure of a dying institution, one which in a few months would be absolutely dead? Rosedale was already rapidly declining in importance; it was no longer an entity with any future. Already many personnel were applying for new community postings, and soon they would be leaving their offices and wards for good, quitting in droves. So Bob benefited on two counts: his dream of a shut-down was now quickly materializing and one of Suzy's blackmailing weapons no longer had any real potency. In fact she knew it was not particularly worthwhile to pursue that line any more. It was useless.

The balance of power was shifting. That realisation of reality's recent reward for him, fickle fate in his favour, was a lovely psychological prize.

A prize for Bob, but a penalty, or more accurately, a punishment, for Suzy. A hefty blow to pierce the armour of her defensive demeanour. The waves of cool complacency which always seemed to be her image rolling forward, now seemed to be in reverse – a rolling backwards. Not now so many icy decisive breakers hitting the beach with her professional power. Her forcefulness was waning, her strategy showing cracks, her big push less and less credible. Most certainly she no longer inspired much charisma in her colleagues, despite her capacity of Rosedale number one. Not many people seemed to respect as before the things she was saying or doing; it was almost as if people were deliberately avoiding her, going out of their way to minimise contact. More crucial still she simultaneously was failing to put the fear of God into others. Nobody felt as if they should humble themselves before her; they were less fearful, less intimidated in her presence.

But from within – her internal resource centre – the things brought up, those things she summoned forth were even more off-putting. Such demons of strategies, conjured up in desperation, gave an impression of an immature, impulsive, insecure instability; her personality appeared decidedly unstable. Such a state of mind was indicative of a pathological condition, not dissimilar from what psychiatrists would quickly and correctly diagnose as psychopathic. A malignant, emotionally superficial state of mind, one both unhealthy and abnormal for anyone who possessed such an antisocial condition, but also one not to be tolerated by other people.

What remaining blackmailing tactics there were clearly came close to scraping the barrel – desperate desires to hurt, wildly inflict wanton pain. The telling of a story to high echelons, and also to Gill Driscoll, about supposed seedy, sleazy, goings on between Daniel, a patient, and Bob, a swearer of the ethically moral hippocratic oath which prohibited such goings on.

Indeed, Bob had easily detected such wild anger in Suzy's red eyes as they had awkwardly conversed on a hospital corridor. Both were cool, despite their obvious antagonism, their actual professional capacities successfully disguising what was really a hot, even boiling encounter. Perhaps it was Bob's calm mood of totally unruffled explanation which put Suzy's powers of self-control to the real test. At some moments she could wildly remove all her clothes, grasp him and take him down with her in her soon-expected downfall. Alternatively, she could feel so outrageously angry as to slap his face with awesome force. But she managed to keep most of her composure, although it was the most difficult thing she'd ever had to do.

She listened, hating every word of his views, every twist and turn of his arguments which she, in advance and to her complete loss, could well anticipate the conclusions. All he said was to her detriment; it was a verbal procession of doom towards her eventual fate, mental burial. But despite all such correctly anticipated gloom she still compelled her ears to remain open and her mouth to remain shut.

Bob had told her that it didn't really cut much ice if she did tell Gill about his bisexual inclinations. Gill had long suspected that anyway. That caused Suzy some anger, but what really stung her the most was the reasons as to exactly why Gill wasn't shattered, in fact more simply a reaction of calm acceptance, even indifference towards revelation. For Suzy was to listen to Bob's explanation of Gill's reaction and, in so doing, realise her own faultiness of emotions.

It went like this. Gill would both understand and accept such a situation precisely because Gill loved Bob, and the meaning of such love was an unselfish committal of Gill to Bob, one both unconditional and no built-in expectations of any necessary reciprocation. Gill had pledged herself years ago into a marriage which she had realistically accepted could go awry, become a problem, but her love for Bob had still guaranteed her a bond to him. So, despite her awareness that it could turn sour, as it in fact now surely seemed, her love overrode that. But, as Bob went on to tell Suzy, it was Suzy's incapacity and inability to genuinely express the emotion of love that was the reason why she couldn't understand Gill's calm acceptance of the situation. For Suzy felt that Gill would be furious, hysterically livid. Suzy expected without any exceptions that all women would act in the same way – as, for instance, with Bob's apparent unfaithfulness, particularly with a person of his own sex. For Suzy White's lack of experience, or more exactly, inability to love someone, led to her always judging or assuming emotional attachments through her narrow telescope of stereotypes.

What her chronic lack of experience – loving experience – had left her was a legacy of distorted vision as to what love really is, how it comes about, what it can mean for two partners who can wonderfully share it. Suzy White's inability to feel, show and share love was the exact reason that she had judged Gill's reaction so incorrectly. Gill was not blazingly furious, for she was capable of love, but Suzy would have been so enraged because, for her, a relationship only existed in the form of a conditional contract, one of reciprocation, not a genuinely unselfish commitment which bears the hallmark of true love.

Chapter Fifteen

Bob Driscoll fatalistically mulled upon rather obscure human misfortune. He was accompanied with Luke in his favourite haunt of the Carrero Café.

Luke sipped lemon tea, trying to dodge the spiralling acrid smoke of his colleague's cigar.

For far from being immersed in a wasteful unimportant mental exercise of unrealism, such a line of lunch hour thoughtfulness was of utmost importance to Bob Driscoll, if not so to anybody else.

Far from toying titillating fancifully, he was attempting, by way of his brilliant imagination, to find a solution to, or at least try to sort out, his current crisis. He used as a start the truth - his vulnerability to physical pleasure of the flesh, sexuality and its power over him, his inability to put a lid upon such arousal, a problem outside his control. One of the very few things which eminent Bob Driscoll couldn't sort out or handle effectively, properly, acceptably, or satisfactorily. Sex was, as he all too alarmingly knew, his only real Achilles' heel.

Daniel Broughton and Reggie Carrero. Two giants of voluptuous, sultry, smouldering prowess. How those two people wound him up incessantly, unsettlingly, played sheer havoc with his worn, torn mind. Hence, although Daniel's mind was actively psychotic, including things such as nightime visitations to hell, with hallucinatory sensations of his burning, his actual body was a full half of the ingredients required for Bob's imaginary hybrid. It was Daniel's smoothness of skin with its white angelic innocence, its unwrinkled timelessness, that sharply contrasted with dark hair of an immortal Egyptian king. More long-lastingly enduring than Tutankhamen.

Danny, king of youth, king of time, king of beauty, master of Bob Driscoll. It was Danny's physical assets, not so much his schizophrenically, unpredictable mentality that was fifty per cent of Bob's desired creation. What then about the other fifty per cent? That which we refer to as one's 'personality'? Most certainly, this was Reggie's ball game – she had that rare magnificence of a mind that was alert and shrewd; hardly ever making a mistake. But to be exact, it wasn't those actual qualities which caused Bob to melt, to succumb, to fall captive to her. Instead it was more subtle than that. It was the sensual vibes or off-shoots of such faculties that Reggie exhibited, due to her precise clever mind, a radiance of dominance. Many men were under such a spell, under her power, her control. That was the key to Bob's helplessness whilst she was ever in his vision, his audible presence, or even his thoughts. For Bob Driscoll liked to be, loved to be, dominated. But for Bob, despite Reggie's considerable good looks, impeccable attire and seductive perfume, this was not the source of her power of domination over him. Instead it was her mind. Her decisiveness, her razor-sharp faculties of decision making, her powers of entrepreneurial judgement, her capacity to hire and fire her employees – all such things and many more caused Bob hormonal turmoil.

He looked at his silent companion who was by now sipping his second cup of tea. Luke spoke first. 'Penny for them,' he said.

'What? My thoughts?' countered Bob.

'Yes.'

'There would be an impossibility of attaching a meaningful price,' said Bob. 'You can't buy dreams.'

'Implying what?' asked Luke.

'Implying I've been thinking bullshit again,' said Bob, lighting another cigar.

'I see,' added Luke. 'You've been thinking of terribly what actually is, and wonderfully of what will never be, yes?'

'You've got it in one,' said Bob with admiration for one of the cleverest, yet modest psychologists he'd ever had the good fortune to meet. Bob continued slowly and in a kind of exploratory way. 'They say that you can't or shouldn't put off things till tomorrow what you can or should do today. What's your rating of that?'

'A piece of misleading folklore, not generalisable, dangerous to individually apply; a largely useless rule of thumb. Why?'

'Because I've hit, or I believe I've hit, one of the nastiest most difficult bits of reality so far - I've never before felt so adrift, confused, unhappy . . .'

'Are you sure it's actually reality you've hit, come to blows with; is reality your true adversary?'

'What do you mean?' questioned a puzzled and worried Bob.

'I mean,' said Luke, 'that you may be fighting illusions, that a lot of all this mess you feel you're in doesn't actually exist - it's *un*reality. You're imagining yourself into all sorts of snares and traps, things that don't necessarily have any relevance to you. You're fighting your own self-built illusions.'

'You're saying that I don't really have too many problems, or those that I think I have aren't real, and that I'm making my life needlessly tough?'

'No, what I'm saying is that all the problems you think you have probably do have an existence in reality, but you're exaggerating their significance unnecessarily.'

'Blowing them up out of perspective?'

'And making them too tangible - giving them too much unwarranted permanence.'

Bob thought that it was a bit reminiscent of his past chats with Doctor Maunders. What on earth was going on? He forced

134

himself to think in a simple, uncomplicated way, then spoke. 'Let's look from a different angle, Luke. Is it a thing we need to rephrase, to study in a different way?'

'Such as?'

'That it's a question of my mistaken belief of there always is a good moment to act, to do something, in contrast to less opportune moments?'

'Ah! The argument of there never being a right time, you mean?'

'Yes.'

'True, I'd say in most cases, for most situations. Yes, that's probably correct, particularly for you at this point in your life.'

'Why particularly for me? And why at this point?'

'Because you're in your mid-life period of transition – a difficult time for lots of guys in their mid-forties; an unsettled, insecure age. Of course for most, as I've just said, it's a classic psychological truism, but it's especially pertinent to you now with the sort of things on your plate.'

'Such as, like what? Drake? Suzy White? Gill? What, exactly?' Luke stared deep into Bob's eyes. 'You've omitted someone.'

'Omitted someone?' Bob asked a little perplexed.

'Yes,' said Luke, still looking deep at Bob's bloodshot eyes. 'You've missed somebody out.'

'Reggie? She's no problem,' Bob hastily countered, waving a hand of confidence.

'I'm not talking about Reggie,' said Luke, 'I'm referring to somebody else. The pivot I believe you're whole frustrations are revolving around, in orbits of irreconcilable pain which they're causing you. Your life, your universe, and the centre of it; you're life-force you've just alluded to.'

It suddenly hit Bob's brain, the mental registration of both self-realisation and also Luke's informed and shrewd awareness. Bob Driscoll almost choked upon the rather stale, dry bread of his sandwich. He thought furiously of whether Luke's honest opinion of Daniel Broughton was one of the main supports of his current crisis, a life crisis, not just crisis of career. Luke continued, the directiveness of his dialogue absolutely point blank. 'Obviously you'd say you love him?'

'Correct,' said Bob a little defensively, a little edgy. 'Quite correct.'

'But at the risk of making your blood boil, might I at least suggest that you've not arrived at and experienced that feeling naturally, that you . . .'

Bob cut his sentence short. 'That I what, exactly? What are you driving at?'

'That you've either uncompromisingly convinced yourself you love him, albeit not any deliberate fault on your part, simply a circumstantial desperation.'

'You're saying I can't objectively, reasonably arrive at a decision, make up my mind?'

'No, now that is a bit unreasonable. I'm simply trying to look at things which are a product of a confused rapid rush of events.'

'So I've been too quick?' Bob said rather annoyed at Luke's attempts of explanation. 'I haven't, in your psychological view, gone about things properly?'

'You have done all things properly, no doubts about it Bob. It's just that there's your total committal that you feel everything is sorted; there are no more things you think should be included.'

'Well, yes, surely that's so, isn't it? What could also be possibly included? I love Daniel, I always will, I feel it deep inside. It's no flimsy infatuation; it's from the heart, Luke.'

'I've never thought otherwise, Bob. Don't get me wrong; your commitment is, I'm certain, total, but . . .'

'But what? But *what?*'

Luke thought for a crucial moment how best to say what he really felt it was time to say, although he knew it wouldn't sound nice, no matter how it was put over. He was trying, as tactfully as possible, to convey something which could quite seriously upset not only a close colleague, but one of his best friends. He decided to be fairly direct and down to earth; for experience had taught him not to beat around the bush in breaking news prone to cause emotional distress.

'You're thinking of your total commitment which I don't dispute, and equally it's also true that it's a full hundred per cent . . .'

'Yes, so what's the problem then?'

'The problem, Bob, is that the figure of a hundred per cent is only your evaluation, your contribution, which is only a net total of fifty per cent in this actual matter.'

'I don't quite understand,' said Bob with a furrowed, anxious brow. 'Explain.'

For perhaps the very first time in over ten years of knowing Bob Driscoll, Luke realised that he had possibly overestimated Bob's mental powers of intellect, even maybe mature common sense.

Bob spoke a little impatiently. 'I'm waiting Luke, waiting for your answer.'

'All right,' said Luke, having now decided to no longer try the 'softly softly' stance. 'You've alluded to the other fifty per cent; you've not considered, and I don't know why not, the other half of it all.'

Bob leaned back in his uncomfortable seat and laughed a bit nervously, a laugh Luke detected may have been false. Bob spoke quickly and it sounded almost apologetic.

'Oh! I see. You think I've not considered Daniel's side! That's the missing fifty per cent, one you think might not fit in with my fifty per cent, yes? You suspect I'm a positive half – willing, committed, but that Danny's not. That's it, isn't it, Luke? You feel I've not taken on board how he might feel about it all?'

'That was part of my argument, Bob, yes, but . . .'

Again Bob cut Luke's sentence short, impatiently, almost

like a pushy, bullying tactic rendering what Luke had to say unfinished.

'Well, as a matter of fact, Luke - and I can say this without attracting any grandiose notions or a sense of arrogance - that Danny is as fully committed to me as I am to him.'

'He's actually told you that?' asked Luke in no uncertain terms.

As it was, Daniel had never actually said anything to Bob about feelings of love, although he had certainly shown a liking, a fondness for Bob's company, and much respect for his advice and generosity. Whether Bob had wrongly embellished Danny's liking for loving, Bob was so confused and stressed he couldn't, for certain, be quite sure. Luke pondered on that - namely, had Bob's anxious recent plight led him to fantasize? Had it all led him to exaggerate Danny's commitment of closeness? Was Bob imagining a happiness which did not, in reality, exist? Was then Doctor Bob Driscoll possibly under the sway of a delusion? Luke knew that the conversation was now one in deep water. It was sensitive; Bob might so terribly easily get hurt as a result, so Luke thought it timely to still stick to the subject but change its emphasis, thereby reducing its intensity. In pursuing such a course it could avoid becoming a heated argument. Bob could get badly offended and hurt; and as Luke was not fully certain of Danny's exact current feelings upon the matter anyway, he decided to go no deeper. It was resembling a session of painful psychoanalysis; one that Luke didn't like, so he tried a refreshingly new angle.

'Correct me if I'm wrong, but Danny's got parole outside Rosedale?'

'Yes, but he rarely uses it,' said Bob.

'Well, how about Danny and myself going for a half day away from it all,' suggested Luke, 'to chat a bit outside the staid routines of the hospital?'

'That's no problem. After all, the staff go on leave, most

138

people in society do, so I don't see why not – anywhere particular in mind?'

'A seaside trip,' suggested Luke, 'despite it being the back end of winter, out of season.'

'When?'

'Tomorrow. There's no security risk and his clinical side's stable. In fact I'm looking forward to it personally.'

'Why, might I ask?'

'Because it seems ages since I had a bit of a break, always being chained to Rosedale meetings in musty rooms, or at my desk in a stuffy office.'

'I feel remarkably similar. Gill and I fly to Sardinia quite soon. We, too, badly need to get away from all this.'

Bob and Luke stood up ready to leave the hot little café, Reggie nowhere in sight. Perhaps she'd gone to another part of her ever-flourishing chain which offered fast food for fast living people in a fast age.

A seagull shrieked and Danny watched its solitary ascent across the grey rooftops of late February Seachester. Down below, solemn green waves kept endlessly, hypnotically, breaking upon a well-nigh deserted beach. Although not bitter or raw, it was a tangy, chilly day, the solitary pier and a lighthouse braving the bashing of the waves.

Luke spoke. 'Have you ever thought about writing a poem about something like this, the unconventional seaside story?'

'As opposed to the usual hot sunny beach of lots of people you mean?' said Danny.

'Yes, no ice cream, swimming gear or deck chairs; just a silent empty greyness, the scene of a sepulchral seaside?'

'I have done already,' replied Danny, still watching the swooping and climbing seagulls. 'Lots of poems and a couple of short stories.'

Luke was a little taken aback, 'So you do creative writing?

I've not seen any of your stuff. Will you show me when we get back? I'd love to read it.'

'It's not really much good,' said Danny. 'The poems don't rhyme.'

'They don't have to,' said Luke. 'In fact, poems that do rhyme are often corny, not so profound as prose.'

Danny was silent for a few moments, his fingers digging into a packet of crisps. 'Let's walk a bit,' he said.

Luke felt that it was the appropriate time to tactfully throw in a few questions. 'I don't suppose it's easy to make lots of friends in a place like Rosedale, is it? A bit of a "passing ships" situation, don't you think?'

'"Acquaintances" is the most it gets to,' Danny replied. 'Like you just said, passing ships.'

'And I should also imagine, seeing that you've done over six years, that you've never really had much chance for lots of friends anyway.'

'I've never had any friends, Luke,' said Danny emphatically. 'I don't know what a friend is meant to mean, or be.'

Apart from finding this sad, Luke considered it intriguing and continued his questions. 'What's your idea of what a friend might be, Danny?'

'Some say it's a person to trust, or enjoy being with.'

'And you don't think that's been your experience at all?'

'No, it's not.'

'I see. So you wouldn't consider Doctor Driscoll to be a close friend, a person who had a liking for you outside of his actual job then?'

Danny tossed his unfinished carton of stewed tea over a wall and watched it fall down to the beach sands. 'I suppose that if I'd had a few girlfriends then I'd never have really bothered with Bob.'

'What does that say for your expectations?'

'It says I need to touch and kiss another human being's body, feel warm skin, and avoid being alone, not having enjoyed sex with girls yet.'

Luke chewed upon this particular comment – it was saying a lot – very relevant for his closest work colleague. 'You mean that Bob's touch is a substitute for a girl's touch, that it's only a sexual release, nothing more?'

'Nothing more, nothing else.'

'So if you'd had some physical fun with females you'd never have wanted Bob's company or even to know him?'

'I guess that's it, Luke,' said Danny fatalistically, a resigned capitulation, a remoteness in his voice. 'Anyway, let's go for a stroll in an amusement arcade, maybe win something.'

Apart from the salty smell of the sea, the sight of seaweed-straddled sand and sound of seagulls, Luke had pleasantly probed, in a sophisticated way, a lot of what he had intended. Luke's skills were quite rare – not just anyone could enquire into the highly personal lives of those highly strung, without inviting accusations of being nosey, too intrusive. Interestingly, Luke had suggested to Danny that he keep a kind of diary – a notebook in which to write his thoughts about Bob Driscoll whenever he felt like doing so. It was a small green notebook and from time to time over coming weeks, Danny put down on paper his various feelings, his conclusions of having known his consultant for six years, in both a formal and informal capacity. The formal – or official – side, of course, being strictly a doctor-patient relationship, one of a purely functional design. But the informal, that is, the more personal or intimate side of it all, was the most important for Luke, inevitably the most important as regards Bob Driscoll's reaction. Luke had tried to consider it from all possible angles, had attempted to sort it out the best way he conceivably could for the hopeful appeasement of all parties concerned. Strangely enough, it was Bob that was Luke's main concern, for Luke had some worry over Bob's recent state of mind and whether or not he could handle stressful events of late; Luke's fear was that Bob might fail to cope. Most certainly, Luke felt Bob could quite easily handle the Drake's and Suzy White's of this world, but a rejection by Danny? Of that Luke had a nagging, gnawing apprehension, a sense of troubled disquiet. This uneasiness was also not going to go away – it was settling in, getting more and more acute. Bob Driscoll's mind needed a rescue operation quite soon, a salvage to prevent possible loss of what people refer to as one's faculties of sanity. Luke was convinced that Bob was approaching breaking point, a point in the shape of a shattering spurning of affection, a point called Daniel Broughton.

As far as Bob Driscoll was concerned, Danny loved him, would continue to do so, never waver from that. Luke Lloyd Evans had often been complimented upon his cool temperament, his calm sense of perspective, his unusual ability to see both sides of people's problems and had invariably managed to effect satisfactory resolutions, acceptable mutual reconciliations. But in this particular case, it was the first time he felt an oncoming crisis of which his efforts would be ineffectual, even futile.

Chapter Sixteen

Suzy White could well have been born in an arid, dry wilderness. A kind of vast desert filled with lots of ladders which pointed up to an occupational sky. Always lots of opportunities to recklessly and ambitiously climb higher and higher. All of the rungs of such career-centred ladders represented people to stand upon, to trample upon, in a blind remorseless advancement. Very few climbers had such brilliant technical skills as Suzy possessed. She often well in the lead, the others straggling, faltering, way behind. It was an arena of a competition of which victory accrued mostly to those contestants without emotional flesh and blood, but instead had minds of cold steel and hearts of uncompromising, gritty sand. People such as Suzy had to often break former ties or connections, no longer useful, ties of the past. Anybody whom she saw as no longer useful or relevant was simply discarded into a waste bin. They had served a purpose, but were since no longer required. Expendable, superfluous faceless figures, all quickly trodden upon, forgotten rungs.

Should then this world's relatively few Suzy Whites be pitied, scorned, praised, ridiculed, smeared, supported or rejected? Perhaps only due to the surprise, the novelty of such a recent unfamiliar phenomenon of female ascendancy of a hitherto masculine mountain was it all such a shock which prompted an uneasy panic reaction in male employees who happened to suddenly find themselves subordinate to and subservient to a woman.

Some say respect is a thing to be earned – perhaps it's true for Ralph Johnson, Bob Driscoll or Luke Lloyd Evans, but it's not so true and has never and probably never will be for an occupationally aspiring Suzy White. For the likes of her it would be doubly difficult, doubly hazardous, and failure doubly painful. Prejudice dies hard. In fact, it doesn't actually ever die, just takes different shapes, surfaces in different forms in the masterful male chameleon of a fictitiously fair world. A fable in which feminists were and are prevented from successfully completing their side of the story.

For one, Suzy White was in dire straits, teetering on a precipice liable to come suddenly crashing hopelessly down. But she was holding on, tenaciously with a grip of steel. Until it happened she would keep climbing, fighting, despite overwhelming opposition. To try was her ambition, to hope was her choice, to flounder was her fate, and to fail in it all was her destiny. Nobody could give a better insight into such a pending demise than Suzy herself, but right now Suzy was preoccupied in the Driscoll household with Gill. Bob was away for a couple of days on an assessment of prisoners who were judged to have deteriorated and might soon be admitted to a psychiatric faculty such as Rosedale.

Suzy offered Gill a cigarette which Gill politely declined.

'It doesn't have to be a show-down,' said Suzy coolly and diplomatically.

'Then what is it?' asked Gill.

'A constructive way of trying to resolve a problem.'

'Whose problem exactly?' enquired Gill, matching Suzy word for word.

Suzy paused, a little bit unprepared for Gill's acuteness. 'Well, mine and yours really; ours, I suppose.'

'Please explain,' said Gill, determined to pin Suzy down, take the sting out of her strategy. 'How precisely do I have a problem? How do you feel we supposedly share a problem? Just what exactly is this super-significant problem you keep hinting at but not actually elaborating upon? Is it perhaps to do with my husband?'

Suzy decided to quit the objective stance, being a little taken aback at Gill's quite formidable intellect. 'Yes, it's about Bob, *all* to do with Bob in fact.'

'And how,' said Gill, 'is that a problem? How is it a problem for me?'

Suzy faltered momentarily, unable, she felt, to outwit Gill, so she tried a little bit of venom in an attempt to maybe prompt an emotional reaction. 'You're aware your husband is no longer quite so faithful but unfortunately in a more strange way than you'd imagine?'

Gill was quite prepared for this knife to be stuck in; she had known for several months, and had suspected it for years. But that wasn't now so vitally important and, although an unpleasant event, the crucial thing was to give Suzy White the full treatment.

'I'm still waiting for an answer, Suzy,' pressed Gill. 'How is all this a problem for me?'

Suzy blew out her cheeks in rising frustration. 'You mean an affair Bob has with one of his own male patients doesn't even affect you, anger you?'

'Certainly it affects me, of course it does, it hurt for quite a long time after Bob let on about it all, but it doesn't anger me. No, in fact I think you're the one that's susceptible to fury, and that you're indulging in what clinicians call projection. A putting onto others your own undesirable feelings, grudges, hang ups and hassles. Am I right?'

Suzy stood up and walked over to a window pretending to show an interest in the distant winking lights of the nearby town. 'Then, from what you're saying, you don't really care much about Bob or yourself any more. I find that unbelievable. For God's sake be open, tell me you're disgusted about it all, bloody outraged.'

'Why should I be feeling that way, Suzy? Can you answer that?' Gill went on. 'As a matter of fact, I can answer that question if you can't. Shall I answer it for you?'

Suzy poured another coffee, her hand a little bit shaky. 'Okay then, why are you so unperturbed that you husband has a rather twisted sexuality and an immoral ethical stance.'

'Because I guess sexual emotions are what we were born with and we cannot directly take responsibility for, whatever, to use your term, *twist* that they might take . . .'

'But—' Suzy interrupted.

'Hold on,' said Gill commandingly, 'I haven't finished yet.'

Suzy sank a bit deeper into her chair and shifted her limbs uncomfortably, uneasily.

'You see,' Gill explained, 'even the travesty of Bob's breach of one of Rosedale's most hallowed ethics is not too much of a shock either. Obviously it's damn serious – people can go to jail for less than what Bob's done and, looked at it that way, of course it's quite devastating, but that's still not the main point I'm driving at, trying to impress upon you. And perhaps the reason you fail to understand is connected to the point itself.'

Suzy outstretched a hand of a gesture of an almost self admitted ignorance. She spoke. 'What then, what is it?'

Gill leaned back and stared at the ceiling then quietly spoke. She was to talk firmly and factually for over five minutes, uninterrupted. In doing so, Suzy White was to receive one of the harshest, yet truest critiques of her life. It appeared that Gill knew an enormous amount about Suzy's psychology, and contrary to Suzy's belief, very little was secret any more. Suzy's baffled incomprehension at Gill's apparent unruffled demeanour as a response to Bob's lifestyle was all made so alarmingly clear to Suzy as she listened, her self consciousness increasing with every word Gill uttered. Suzy's bitterness was a reflection of a complex core of a serious personality disorder – one which had its roots in Suzy's actual perspective upon her distorted sense of self-entitlement, coupled with an insatiable need to exact recognition. She felt it imperative to be not just in a spotlight, but to remain in such a centre stage position in order for her particular existence to be meaningful. Suzy could never accept a marginal place, a backstage part in the world. She virtually had to be the biggest star in the show, a show which must run throughout her life, and never waning in its popularity or audience capacity.

It was her self-centredness of a rapidly spreading envy which was poisoning any balanced perspective upon her life. Such an attack upon her horizons of a waning normality was giving an unhealthy psychiatric state. Suzy White might quite easily have been mentally ill for several years – totally unnoticed, undetected by herself. For despite her powers of insight, upon the issue of her own sanity she was completely unaware of such a condition. If it was a fault of somebody, her pride would never had admitted personal failure; rather it would be someone else – such as Bob Driscoll. Because he didn't love her she felt it was his fault, namely that he must love her; Suzy White simply didn't understand love.

But it didn't quite end at a simple summing up or amateur, though correct, diagnosis of Suzy by Gill Driscoll. For Gill went on to say why, in Suzy's actual case, it had so little chance of all being put in an optimistic mode of reverse – why Suzy had maybe left a cure a bit too late. At this revelation, a red-faced, exasperated and shattered Suzy White could only listen as Gill Driscoll hammered in the final nails in a coffin of reason for Suzy's imminent demise. For, said Gill, if Suzy had ever managed to possess or develop the human capacity to love other than merely ogle, lust for or desire, then with a bit of time and self-insight, a cure for her impending illness might have been possible. An impending breakdown could have been prevented. Yet such a hope was dashed with Suzy's metallic heart, in fact a psychopathic condition lacking emotional identification, an empathy for other people's feelings. Gill got deeper still in cleverly showing another facet of the complex crisis Suzy was acutely suffering from. It was ironically Suzy's abilities of intellect and insight into certain parts of her disorder which subconsciously allowed her to be so privately disgusted with her faults. Suzy knew in a way that not everybody else was to blame but kidded herself that they were. She had successfully managed to delude herself. Gill added to her observation that it was a very rare condition or type of disorder – that of a hundred per cent self-compliance in the tragic and pitiful manufacture of a paradoxically much-dreaded demise. At that Suzy didn't need any more strong coffee; instead strong alcohol and a totally clean sweep of all she was doing at Rosedale and all the people there.

Suzy had an urgent drive to get out of the psychiatric system altogether, for if she didn't go very soon, then she knew she would be in a place like Rosedale not as medical director, but as an acutely distressed patient on an admission ward.

Gill Driscoll showed Suzy out into the cold evening and Suzy slowly walked to her recently acquired company Jag. Her face felt extremely hot and her mouth was dry, her heart racing beneath her ribcage, almost breaking out after the successive shocks of Gill's cutting criticisms. Suzy set the controls of her mind towards drafting an immediate statement of formal resignation as she set the path of the car towards her Rosedale office. It was raining heavily, the wipers futile to stop a blurred watery windscreen, and Suzy was deep in thought, admitting defeat. For her, at least, this was a definite Armageddon – the final reckoning had arrived. If feminism had failed at all, it had failed for her; as far as Rosedale hospital was concerned or places similar, the twentieth century organization woman was dead.

Chapter Seventeen

Bob Driscoll blew out his crimson sunburned cheeks and stared up at the blue roof of the Mediterranean. He shifted in an uncomfortable deckchair whilst Gill sipped an iced lemon drink. Two weeks away; a holiday of sorts, away from grey, drab England's back-end of a bad winter. The sunshine, however bright, was not so easily successful in lifting his seriousness, his almost abject depression. The resort of Santa Marguerita da Paula at Sardinia's southernmost tip all seemed so full of people enjoying themselves.

Gill spoke first. 'It doesn't necessarily have to be like this. Us, that is. You could easily have a total change of career.'

'I doubt it, Gill,' Bob said rather flatly, a lack of ambition or effort in his reply. 'I guess I'm stuck now with an ill-chosen destiny.'

'And what about me?' asked Gill, a slight tone of irritable insistence in her question, which was perhaps due to her awareness that what was happening to Bob's crumbling career had direct, perhaps bad repercussions for her quality of life.

'I suppose,' Bob said, 'we'll drift apart in a slow painless way. At least we've tried – *and* had lots of good times until recently. Anyway, let's relax, okay?'

Let's relax. Those glib, almost infuriating spoken words with a subtle hint telling Gill to shut up, not carry the dialogue any further. She looked at her husband, cigar smoke leaving his mouth in blue wisps. Let's relax. How his recent capitulation to a bad patch angered her, made her madly wish in so many ways that they'd never married at all. Let's relax. How on earth could she? How could she put up blinds to shut out a reality that was destroying his mind, crippling what little happiness she had left remaining? Yet, despite her intermittent flashes of anger, her indignation at his fatalism, she felt that incredibly it might still work out all right.

As she sat there liberally applying lotion to her flesh, she wondered if having children might have altered the situation, would have made it all any better. She wasn't sure, and didn't ask him, as he sat there staring upwards at a plane with its white smoke leaving a trail high in the sky. She wondered what he was thinking about, but again didn't ask.

Bob was thinking, with a nauseating shiver – despite being in the boiling noon-day heat – of what, for him was now a forsaken doomed Rosedale hospital. All remnants of what a hospital should ideally be were absent, in his opinion; Rosedale was virtually nothing now, didn't mean anything to him any more. He thought of twelve days from now touching down on the miserable tarmac of a British airport runway, back to the sickening plight of reality he wanted to cut himself away from, and was indeed succeeding in doing.

Gill broke the silence. 'I'll pop to the site shop and get some postcards and lemonade.'

'Yes, I'm going in to shower soon anyway,' he said, and closed his eyes.

As Gill walked off into the distance he opened his eyes again and looked at Gill strolling through the heat. The temperature was a good thirty degrees Centigrade and reflected a painful white brightness to one's eyes. The haze made a fluid phantasmagoric shape of Gill as she walked further away, a shrinking surrealism of a dwindling figure. Bob decided to go into the 'all mod-cons' villa to cool off. He might have appeared a bit abrasive to Gill, but before even reaching the shower, his own unhappy mental trap had him bursting into a confused bewilderment of tears.

Gill was also somewhat misty-eyed, trying in vain to hide her melancholia from all the other tourists in the shop, those that all seemed to be smiling, laughing, full of sun.

The evening was cool, the fierce afternoon inferno drained out of the day. The sand was soft underfoot, Bob strolling in a pair of shorts, a wad of several thousand lire stuffed into a back pocket. There was so much they could so very easily say, but somehow it no longer seemed relevant, important. Bob's eyes fixed upon a couple of dark-haired youths kicking a ball about, and it reminded him of Daniel. Gill looked knowingly at her husband's enthralled face, his mouth agape. She suggested they go for something to eat as she suddenly felt hungry. She knew that Bob, too, was quite hungry as he stared at the youths, but not hungry for food, and not any longer particularly hungry for her either. They made a turn towards a night restaurant, one which other tourists said was too expensive, with wine too warm and the fish usually off. But it didn't put the Driscolls off. As they slowly sauntered past villas in the dimness of a silent dusk Bob began to chat openly, more freely. Gill, too, seemed without any inhibitions.

Rather sadly they reminisced over twenty years of their union, one which started out as a wonderful coloured flower which nothing could taint or prevent from blossoming into a radiant flourish of promise. They remembered how it all imperceptibly, but ironically, had quite violently taken a cruel, totally unforeseen and vicious twist. All the early harmony poisoned, the freshness so blandly staled due to a career wreaking untold cancerous damage to their contentment. They'd been psychologically assaulted, wounded, beaten black and blue over recent years.

'What do you think it was, Gill – the specific turning point?'

'You mean the event that caused our mutual ruin?' she said.

'Yes. What the hell do you think such a demon was?'

A demon, Gill thought; such a metaphor may be a little odd, a reference or description of misfortune Bob wouldn't usually make, a comment which could more easily be attributed to his patients, with their delusional accounts of their breakdowns. Still, Gill dismissed her concern and added some imagery of her own to give a possible answer.

'A dark alley of circumstance accountable to no one; one we unluckily walked down. Our love burgled, our fortunes manhandled, our bond victimised. We've both had a bad bruising.'

'I suppose it's all down to two things, really. Realism and one's connected expectations. That's what you could call a gamble on an unknown future, your ideally hoped for lifestyle.'

'And whether it comes off nice or nasty is up to circumstantial whim of luck or bad luck; its called, perhaps, the dubious privilege of having a life.'

'I'd add it's unfairly dubious – we didn't choose birth or its implications, still the word "fair" is superfluous as a human term, anyway. Burgers, hot dogs or chips? What snack do you fancy?' said Bob, changing from his philosophy to talk trivia.

'Hot dogs would be nice,' she said, gazing at the completely still waters of the outdoor swimming pool. No ripples at all, just unbroken, silent, still dark water. 'That's a sharp contrast from this afternoon, isn't it?' she asked.

'You mean the mid-afternoon splashing of people ducking and diving?'

'Yes, a pool of activity. Something that was alive.'

'But, I take it, you now think dead?'

'Perhaps; a bit like our journey for twenty years. What do you think about it?'

'I think the whole nub of it all is we, or possibly me more than you, have done far too much thinking. Thinking instead of spontaneously doing; studying life, not enough living of it.'

'Good. I think that's what I've long suspected, not just of you but us both, as well as all the Rosedale rank and file; we've analysed simplicity, thought all of our pleasure into useless oblivion. We've speculated ourselves into a dingy attic full of books, but an attic of so few people.'

'Psychiatry does that to anyone who has the guts to practice it; you analyse yourself to death, never stop thinking, even of whether your funeral is a normal or appropriately planned act. I need to see the back of psychiatry, and the bulldozers ramming Rosedale into extinction. You can get a junior registrar in your office on a contract for six months and all he does is put patients on drugs, collects a salary, then at the end of the six months, suddenly goes to some other place – and all that's happened is he's prescribed confusion.'

'So consultants can provide a good recipe for chaos?'

'And worse,' Bob said dogmatically, lighting a small cigar. 'But some wonderful therapy can be thought of in an imaginary way when we extend our idea of the asylum.'

'What it might mean in a wider sense?'

'Absolutely, and not too far away from late twentieth century reality.'

'How it all ties in with life, everyone's lives?'

'And suffering especially; that and death.'

'How exactly?'

'That death itself has a massively tangible form, even though invisible to us whilst alive. Once dead, death shows itself not as blackness, not a void, not a vacuum; above all, death is certainly anything but a sensation of nothingness. It's form is very real, and surprisingly familiar at least to those acquainted with asylums.'

'Death is an asylum?'

'It certainly is, Gill. Asylum literally means a sanctuary, a tranquil place of undisturbed peace and rest.'

'For the crippled minds of all of us who have had a bad deal whilst alive?'

'All of us. Everyone gets battered, their souls shattered, hopes knackered; this life knocks the stuffing out of all who exist – our dubious fate we spoke of . . .'

'What are the details of death as an asylum? What's on offer as a cure – speaking in metaphors of fantasy?'

'No fantasy; metaphors, may be about our grim reaper, but no fantasy; death is as real, as true, as substantial as life. But it goes one better; it's a resting place forever.'

'Just a tolerance for us of three score and ten in this hell of a life, then an immortal hospitalisation?'

'Yes, death is a great healer. Death doesn't need to worry about time; it's got loads and loads of time. It's got eternity. Death is eternity, immortality and hence, we can then refer to heaven.'

'The asylum of recovery and ultimate rest being synonymous with heaven?'

'Well, what does it sound like to you? A bit too deep? A ramble by your unfaithful husband due to too much wine? Crap talk? What, I ask you,' said Bob, 'do you make of it all and most of all – me?'

'I love the man I married, love him always through life and now I can add due to your explanations, right through death; our mutual rest, the asylum of eternal recuperation. We both need such a rest, don't you think?'

'Yes,' said Bob, draining another glass of wine. 'We bloody well do!'

It was now very dark and still, the calm night broken only by an occasional chatter of crickets. Gill was in the villa bedroom undressing, washing away perspiration of an enervating, energy-sapping hot day. Bob was sitting thoughtfully outside on the porch, chain smoking and drinking himself into insensibility. Gill was very confused – all of tonight's chat was with a man she had recently come to view, not just with concern, but with a worried anxiety. For over twenty long years he'd never spoken in such a way, and it didn't, no matter what he'd said tonight, in any way go towards preventing their crisis and the imminent divorce. He'd not spoken about Danny Broughton at all, just a philosophical monologue which, no matter how moving or inspiring, was totally unrelated and unhelpful to their actual difficulties. Yet still Gill wouldn't give in. She switched off the main bedroom light and switched on two small pink lamps. She looked into the wardrobe mirror. She had always believed in God and prayed to him now. 'Make me look young again, as I once was.'

She lay naked under the thin sheet waiting nervously but with some conviction; a desperate desire to stop the rot, salvage something, prevent Bob from sliding into maybe a permanent mental breakdown. Suddenly the bedroom door whined open as Bob staggered slowly and clumsily in, the door whining shut. Neither spoke as he climbed with difficulty into the bed.

For a few minutes he felt sick with her clammy lips and hands upon his skin, then their breathing slowed and Gill fell quickly asleep. But Bob just lay there, drunk but awake, staring up at the ceiling. He thought of a crazy biography and no apparent end. He tried to remember the things he'd said this evening to her but couldn't, and assumed he'd just merely shelved the problem, the crisis they were in, and that he'd talked a lot of crap, alcohol-induced nonsense. He looked at Gill's sleeping face and thought of the two dark-haired youths he'd seen earlier on the beach and their resemblance to Danny. A guilty but sad prod hit his mind, that he'd not only wasted the best of his life in a stupid, useless career, but had also wounded Gill; betrayed a good woman's love.

Such a miserably tainted vacation for Bob had its twin reflection in glaring, frightening lights of a Rosedale theatre for psycho-surgery. The bright lights caused scalpels to shine, and lots of other strange ultra-sharp metal instruments to catch reflections of what was a watershed in the biography of Danny Broughton. Whilst Bob sipped beer in the shade, Danny lay still, anaesthetized, in a white gown upon an operating table. A big event in that Danny was involuntarily waving goodbye to half a personality, on a permanent basis. A physical loss of memory retention which Bob Driscoll knew nothing of.

How had it come to this nightmarish spectre? What had happened whilst Bob soaked up the sun and dwelled upon an unhappy life he wished he'd never lived? Why, as soon as Bob took a holiday, did Doctor Drake of all people assume responsibility for Danny's care? It was the case that Doctor Driscoll, the senior Rosedale consultant, had many times insisted emphatically that none of his own caseload of patients ever be under the responsibility of Drake in his absence.

Slowly the thin blade made almost a circular incision upon Danny's right temple. A thin stream of dark red blood trickled down Danny's face and neck, immediately swabbed by a rather frosty-faced young surgeon whose job it was to wash instruments, apply bandages and, of course, swab up any blood. Doctor Richardson, the senior cerebral surgeon, was now carefully attempting to finely separate and divide up a mass of tissue of nerve tracts. If this was successful, then supposedly the patient concerned would have a much milder temperament, a greatly reduced capacity for aggression. But aggression in Daniel Broughton's case? Surely it could not be. Danny was not violent, had shown no recorded propensities to harming anybody, not even threatening anyone. But all that, whether true or not, was now eclipsed by the actual action taken; that based upon and acted upon directly on the recommendation of Doctor Drake. The bandages were now being applied, a small metal plate sewed upon the hole made by the incisions. The trolley and Danny, unconscious upon it, was slowly wheeled to the sick bay dormitory, the recovery suite.

Doctor Drake had interviewed Danny and was quite categorical that medication was not the required solution, nor electric shocks; but a minor psycho-surgical operation could do the trick. Promptly, Drake made his views explicit to surgeons who were bound to act upon his recommendations. They could not dispute his views, even if they wished.

Bob Driscoll and Daniel Broughton were completely unaware of all this horror – Danny would probably never be able to even remember or recall the atrocious speed with which he had been so unprofessionally, scandalously and undeservedly leucotomised. Maybe the term 'leucotomised' was a super-Rosedale euphemism for being brutally victimised; it seemed Drake had scored with his amazingly unaccountable savagery once again. After all, his neatly typed recommendations upon the surgeon's desk were of a brevity which reflected his brutality: 'Frontal leucotomy may render greater personality passivity and accordant stability. In consequence, there will be a reduction in intensity of distress, anxiety and occasional bouts of hostility towards others. No doubt such a procedure would be supported by Doctor Driscoll, Mr Broughton's regular consultant, currently on leave. No additional comments are deemed, in this particular case, to be necessary.'

Chapter Eighteen

Hardly agreeable. More akin to a diabolically vituperative
vendetta. An antagonism of a cauldron of fiery anger of Bob
Driscoll's most ugliest of hates. It would now be no longer a
mere professional contretemps of clinical disagreements, not
even great distaste – instead it was Doctor Driscoll's passion to
destroy Doctor Drake's career, have him struck off the psychiatric
register for ever.

All this would come for the reason it had to do, for satanic
and sinister gurus like Drake should not be permitted to practice
medicine in grotesque Mephistophelean ways. Bob would see
to it – the humiliating fate of Doctor Drake.

Bob Driscoll only had to look at the cabbaged wretch in
bandages he'd for so long deeply felt more affection for than
anybody else upon earth. Those blood-stained bandages around
a victimised skull. The vacant, reality vagrant expression gazing
into space, oblivious to Bob's voice or the ticking sickbay clock.
The last rays of a winter sun, cutting through the windows, fell
in weak lemon light upon Danny's bed. Danny looked no longer
at Bob but through him; there seemed in Daniel a torpor of
inability to any longer register incoming stimuli, be it of sound,
sight, touch or smell. Just a void of sensory receptivity; it was
like trying to talk to, catch the attention of, or elicit the response
from a piece of furniture. Danny Broughton was now a piece
of wood, emotionally stripped, robbed, deprived.

Bob placed a cigarette in the zombie's hand, a loose hand

which failed to grasp, and the cigarette simply dropped onto the cold linoleum floor. Bob couldn't stand much more of this bizarre nightmare. In a moment he'd leave, for if he remained he'd certainly plunge into unavoidable and uncontrollable sobs over something almost dead.

But Bob's love was too strong. Even a robot could be madly adored. Bob would continue to love him. Even a robot could approximate to being human; so long as Danny's heart kept beating, Bob would always be close, even if the brain was permanently wounded.

Bob quietly, but quickly, left the dormitory, his departure unnoticed by an almost unseeing, unmoving Daniel. Bob needed to unclutter his buzzing mind, deluged as it was by a thousand conflicting, nagging thoughts. He decided to stroll in the frosty hospital grounds, the sharp fresh air hopefully dispelling an unwanted thickness of cobwebs.

It was a late March afternoon, a pale sun darting between ragged yellow clouds. It was peaceful. Nature seemed to have a nakedness about it, an unbroken seal of unspoilt newness. Such a virgin gladly welcomed his slow footsteps through the frost. Bob thought that these peaceful grounds had already reached the age of well over a hundred years, had seen so many bright summers, so many sad winters. He stopped next to a long disused water fountain, a victorian relic for thirsty lunatics, all now long dead. He dwelt upon such a point, extending its seemingly non rational argument. Is the only real cure for mental disorder, the only *permanent* cure simply death? Is dying as yet the only solution to all the poor wretches so unfortunate to fall into an asylum catchment net? If that was so, all the battery of drugs and other psychiatric paraphernalia were all well-nigh useless – just an excuse for a profession that should never exist, a body of practitioners who should never be.

He stubbed out his cigar on the fountain looking up at the upper floors of red brick and twisted convoluted drainpipes, here and there the occasional gargoyle. He walked on, still somewhat morbidly retaining his picture of death. Was all this white frostiness a fitting shroud for Rosedale, very soon a victim of remorseless bulldozers? A levelling of a brick and iron obscene testimony of man's inhumanity to man? A century-old secret all hidden within the four crumbling perimeter walls, a successful conspiracy by way of political and economic exigency of the lack of humane tolerance to society's less fortunate members.

Bob felt almost as if he could cry. Looking at all this unrushed peacefulness of the silent beautiful grounds, the white wonderland. Yet, he knew just two floors above all this lovely tranquility was the reality of the sick bay - and the terrible crime it contained - an innocent victim of a surgical knife. A mental outlook of former clarity turned, after unjustified tinkering, into a vegetable - an unresponsive statue. For one moment Bob Driscoll wondered if Danny's future was a worthwhile future - if he'd be better off dead; but Bob guiltily, and rapidly, dismissed such a cruel reflection. Bob also wondered what Drake was doing right now. Perhaps he was at some glorified modern psychiatric consortium lecturing lots of eager medical students upon the more human changing face of western psychiatric services to clients. For such a travesty, Drake would be paid as much as a thousand pounds for a couple of afternoon lectures. How could Bob get back at Drake, nail him? What would really hurt, sting Drake the most? Not money. Drake was quite rich. Not a demotion either. Bob wanted to completely decimate Drake's career for good; to prevent Drake ever being legally allowed to have any connection with psychiatry again. That was the best attack, it would cripple Drake because, in a crazy way, Drake loved this job, despite his unsuitability for it. He would not be able to fall into another career easily - as the only thing he had qualifications and contacts in was his present slot of forensic psychiatry.

Bob lit a cigarette and looked out across a thick mistiness of

the now darkening afternoon, shivered in the encroaching chill
and went back inside.

Chapter Nineteen

When Bob Driscoll drew fifty thousand pounds from the bank, the cashier didn't bat an eyelid, for the polite ever ready-to-please clerk knew Bob's financial status – the sum just drawn was only six months' earnings, if that. Fortunately, Bob had a couple of fairly free days, and was utilizing them to the full. Hence, the nine-thirty first bank customer and then the first telephone call for Jim Holland at his *Mercury* office.

'We're not beating about the bush any more,' said Bob calmly but decisively.

'From the sound of your voice and the very early call I can see that,' said Holland.

'In fact, I'm winding up lots of bits and pieces, cleaning up my part of a disorderly Rosedale career, and believe me, it's as tatty as hell.'

'But, thinking back to our previous chats, that's always been your opinion on the place hasn't it?'

'Afraid so. But now, before the place starts to teem with demolition workers, I need to get some important stuff sorted out, in particular a kind of burial . . .'

'Burial?'

'Clifford Drake's funeral – not a literal service though, because much to my regret he hasn't as yet died but I'd still like him buried; I'd like the profession I'm in to feel his absence, his exodus. Okay?'

'Fine with me. If you remember the *Mercury*'s already got

lots of little gems about your place, as well as damning indictments of Doctor Drake.'

'Good dirty stuff?'

'It couldn't be much blacker. Have you any more shit to help crucify him as well as put him under the ground?'

'I have, and as a matter of fact, it's largely undisclosed – nobody, even my close medical colleagues, know about it. It's true as well. If it was printed he'd not only be out on his ear pronto, he'd maybe land in jail.'

'What?'

'It's going back many years when Drake was barely qualified, and what happened wasn't in this country either.'

'Where? This is new stuff.'

'It happened in a secure psychiatric unit in New York. He dropped one hell of a clanger.'

'Drake's practised abroad? In the United States?'

'Yes, with an appalling catalogue of errors.'

'Never knew that. And what dropped him in it over there, then?'

'He out-stepped his situation, his professional judgement, and was sacked and sued, and the only way he could continue in psychiatry was to practise over here. America wouldn't tolerate him. I'm surprised we ever did. He well-nigh killed a young woman.'

'How? Again this is an eye opener, all fresh to the *Mercury*. It could be our biggest article for ages. How did he almost kill this woman?'

'Well, you know Drake's always been obsessional, crazy about dishing out ECT – electric shock treatment – yes? Well, some doctors have the mistaken idea that a patient benefits from ECT more if not anaesthetized.'

'You mean electrically shocked whilst still fully conscious?'

'Exactly. And also not given any drugs or muscle relaxants either.'

163

'What's the upshot? One not too pleasant, I would imagine.'

'A wave of excruciating pain when the current's shock hits the patient's brain, a part of a tongue probably bitten off due to the convulsion induced and, often due to the seizure, broken, disjointed bones. It's long since been legally ruled out in the States, but that was after Drake's episode.'

'What actually happened to the woman he shocked without anaesthetic then?'

'She's lying flat on a hard bed for ninety per cent of her remaining days. A shocked spinal distortion. She's never been able to walk since. Drake had to pay lawyers nearly every cent he had to avoid a stink, to just about cover it all up.'

'Then what in God's name is he still doing in the bloody job and being allowed to get away with in Rosedale? He's using the same sort of rough 'treatments' he got kicked out of the States for.'

'That's always been my biggest and very personal axe to grind: professionalism and its legal and medical aloofness, its abuses barely open to outside criticism. It's a law unto its own in forensic medicine, and that makes me extremely annoyed; that's why I'm ringing you about that sort of thing at this time of the morning. It's bugging me, and I can't mentally put it to one side. I need to sort it out.'

'How would you like the format?'

'Hold on a moment, there's another thing. You and Frank, your boss, have an unexpected bonus – fifty grand coming your way if this really sells.'

'Fifty grand for me and Frank. Why?'

'Because it means a lot to me. A lot of things have been recently taken away from me. I need now, with press help, to do a bit of taking away myself, to do a little bit of destruction.'

'Such as damaging Clifford Drake?'

'You've got it in one, Jim.'

'Was it anything really personal, or was it simply professional disagreements?'

'Both. But much more of a personal thing; either way, the guy shouldn't even exist.'

'After all he's done?'

'After all he's destroyed.'

'Pretty powerful stuff. I like it, front and middle pages guaranteed. Any photos?'

'Not necessary, but maybe a few good shots of Rosedale might help, and try and include that ugly perimeter wall.'

'A grim story of a grim place, yes?'

'As grim as grim can be.'

'Leave that up to me. There's a lot I have been busting to have said about all this myself. I tried once with a daft social worker; got taken for a ride.'

'You shouldn't have bothered with Dave Harrison or his department. They're unacquainted with rough stuff; they're too academic, soft, meek. All do-gooders without any mud on their shoes, and blood on their hands. You don't often see a social worker cry.'

'What do you mean by that?'

'They're far too refined, always a sideline stance. They apply a sociology textbook to very real hurt hearts and minds.'

'And the result I can well imagine.: they analyse suffering, study people to death.'

'Yes, then they move on to yet another institution and simply repeat the pity-a-poor-patient syndrome.'

'And of course they're getting paid for that on tax-payers' money. The tax-payer's a productive citizen; the social worker, the parasite on the tax-payer, the social sponge.'

'And social scourge.'

Bob was feeling more buoyant now that his long awaited chance had arrived, but there was something very disappointing, something Jim Holland had told him which cheesed him off, albeit for only a few hours. It was a bit of what could be called a tabloid technicality, a situation which most newspapers often come up against and find to their displeasure. It was something not usually known outside the modern media world, and it was of a nature such as to affect Bob Driscoll's strategy of a Rosedale revelation. Jim explained the pros and cons of it, gave Bob the score. It was a kind of win and lose situation, and it presented Bob with a difficult dilemma. He'd patiently kept in the pipeline two key objectives: one, of course, of ruining Drake, but also another goal which was very important to him – a Rosedale exposure. He wanted the public to see the indecent exposure of a disgustingly obscene institution, actually witness it of newspaper print. The long overdue revelation of an out of place dinosaur, a psychiatric anachronism. This was where Bob found himself at a difficult crossroads.

For, as Jim Holland explained, both objectives could not be met; it was a case of one or the other. Bob couldn't have a Drake exposure as well as a Rosedale revelation because if both stories were printed at roughly the same time, then either's force of sensationalism would detract from the other, due to two competing items of news. If both were printed simultaneously, as Bob would ideally wish, then ironically their effectiveness would be reduced – less impact than if just one story were printed. To that apparent problem Bob suggested to Jim that a solution would be to space the stories out, do them both but with an interval, a few days in between. Yet again, as Jim explained to Bob's disappointment, that seemingly simple strategy wouldn't work either. For as Frank Farley, Jim Holland or any news reporter is only too well aware from press experience, there is the crucial rush for time for a paper to meet deadlines. Such a sense of rushing, of having to get a story and print it as soon as possible is due to competition – either real or imagined – from other newspapers, which are sniffing around the same kind of story. An almost infectious atmosphere of media paranoia, competition giving an escalating fear of being pipped to the post, too late to get a story in first. Especially an exclusive article. The press cannot wait, each rival paper uncertainly suspicious, always looking over its apprehensive insecure shoulder at another paper, whose reporters are doing just the same thing. First and foremost, a paper's staff have the paramount objective to gain the highest circulation figures; the newspaper is in business to sell papers. A criterion well down the paper's list of priorities is whether or not some item they print happens to be true or not; truth is not really important. What is crucial is to sell more papers than any rival, to out-do other media competitors.

So, as Jim was at pains to impress upon a somewhat subdued Bob Driscoll, the story would have to be of a *Mercury* exclusive – out on sale. Front and centre pages as soon as was possible, as early as practicable. Even the actual quality of the article didn't need to be a classic impressive piece of English literature; that didn't matter. What did matter above all else, was that the *Mercury* got in first. Any delays, even so much as a matter of a couple of hours and the *Clarion*, the *Herald* or even the more sombre restrained papers like *The Times* could creep in and steal a promising big selling story. The less time to play with the better.

Regrettably, a long-time employee in a high position in Rosedale, Doctor Driscoll had to bite his lip. He could not, by way of media assistance, blow the lid off Rosedale, blow the whole roof off traditional crude hit or miss psychiatry. But in a way, that no longer really mattered any more. The radical shake-ups or reorganisation in the British Health Service would amply do the job for Bob.

Once a death knell of the institution had been heard, Bob would probably slot himself into freelance, flexible work, no longer part of a chain of command or a board of directors to have to listen to and obey when he so often felt like violently disagreeing. No more bureaucracy epitomized in the shape of a company hierarchy stifling any self-initiative, paralysing of imagination. So, in a rather weird way, it was as if Bob too had been imprisoned, held against his will in a system he'd so long grown to dislike. He, too, would be away very soon from Rosedale. He would soon be free as well. Yes, he felt he'd always stay close to Danny, and pay off any legal monies to Gill as a result of impending divorce. And yes, he'd remain in his first love of jobs – helping those mentally unfortunate, but no longer within asylum walls, but out in the community. That, he felt, was the most pivotal point in his occupational life so far, and of course he felt he still had another pleasant gift, Daniel Broughton, for many happy years to come.

For Danny's leucotomized damage of his personality did not put off Bob's enthusiasm one bit. In fact, it drove Bob even closer to him, to be more committed. This was due to Bob's unstinting perseverance for the unfortunate underdog, those victims of the forensic medical system. Bob was now starting to bounce back with a relish, a rejuvenation of commitment to all his obligations and responsibilities towards others. He was feeling fairly certain that his recent life crisis was on the way out, that on all fronts things had picked up favourably and could only get better.

That was how Bob perceived it. He saw a renewal of former, much-missed powers of self-control, those which had been sadly relinquished through circumstantial fate.

But a side-line cynic, a neutral, insightful observer, might not have the same comfortable stance as Bob now reassuringly felt. Opinions could be widely diverging, Bob's complacency of a cocoon being not quite so safe at all, but an unlucky ill-fated bomb shelter. He could be huddled into a false sense of security, on borrowed time, seconds slipping away before the whole rosy image – the dream – was blown to kingdom come.

Such a destiny might await Bob Driscoll, another destiny might await Drake. Already, even without the imminent deluge of publicity, Bob was more or less certain that not only was it a lifelong exodus from anything remotely resembling the occupation of medicine, but that Drake could soon be sued, made bankrupt – a pauper, a ghost of a former figure of prestige; a tramp of a rogue, a sinister apparition that sleeps under bridges, upon park benches, never tastes the light of anything worthwhile again. That punishment should be meted out to Drake for the simple reason that he was not worthwhile as a person, and as far as most Rosedale personnel were concerned, he was worthless, not worth anything at all, and never would be ever again.

Perhaps criminal proceedings would be taken against him by eminent lawyers, acting for aggrieved relatives of the patients his so-called treatment had so hideously distorted. A bad man. An evil man. A ruthless, arrogant, inept, incompetent, embarrassment for the psychiatric profession, best kicked into obscure oblivion. An oblivion of a netherworld, a Hades of a fiery, forsaken wasteland, fit only for those such as Drake to crawl through in disgraceful purgatory of eternal hell. Such was Drake's fate.

Bob Driscoll was in total support of all such happenings and welcomed changing psychiatric procedures and organization. A case of a long-awaited 'out with the old in with the new'.

One mid-morning there was an extra bit of good news from Trish Turner, the Rosedale public relations trouble-shooter, and long-time friend of Bob.

'It would,' said Trish, sitting opposite Bob in the busy canteen, 'have meant a Rosedale closure anyway.'

'Even if there were no initiatives for community care?'

'Absolutely,' Trish replied confidently. 'You see, the Health Department and Home Office were aware of Rosedale, much more than you or I ever thought.'

'The Drakes' and Suzy Whites' malpractices, for example?'

'Yes, and the bungling, dithering Ralph Johnson, and so much more.'

'Who do you think was doing the leaks, all the undercover informing?'

'Mainly patients' relatives, that via legal advisers.'

'That's sad,' said Bob.

'Why?'

'Because it's the same old story, reminiscent of a hundred years of institutional damage inflicted upon powerless patients, and such evils only coming to light after patients' relatives fought for, campaigned so hard for, an elimination of such abuse – by way of complaint – to those up top. Patients' relatives who were, and are, paid not a penny for such efforts to remove institutional malpractices, abuses, bad treatment of patients who are powerlessly confined in such obscene institutions. That being the case it should be the Suzy Whites or Ralph Johnsons who should be removing and stamping out such horrible things. It is their paid employment, their responsibility to directly do so. It shouldn't have to be a patient's sister, wife, mother or uncle that has to write out letters of complaint to the health division in London. It should be the task of officialdom in the actual institution itself.

'I blame the bone idle, ineffectual, parasitic good-for-nothings like Ralph-comfy-life-Johnson or that awful bitch Suzy White! God! How I've grown to hate this place!'

'You seem quite upset and angry about it all, Bob. Is there anything about Rosedale you find worthwhile, anything or anybody worth salvaging or retaining?'

Bob's eyes momentarily gleamed through a now passing mistiness. Yes, there was something, or more exactly somebody, who was worth clinging onto, worth salvaging in this ugly Rosedale sea; someone Bob felt was forever worthwhile, very beautiful. But he couldn't at that moment, bring himself to tell Trish. It was all too much.

Chapter Twenty

Spring had exploded away any remains of what had been a seemingly interminable, dragging winter. The daffodils proudly bloomed as they had always done in the Rosedale grounds for over a century, during all those previous Aprils, long-forgotten blossomings of an irrecoverable past. Bob and Luke stared out at the gardens as they sat in a porch of the young offenders section of Rosedale hospital – a hospital whose funeral was being arranged, a hum of a bulldozer nearby.

Bob spoke. 'A century of secrets, pleasure and pain, confusion and disillusion, all coming to a close.'

'A timely, long-overdue close, don't you think?' said Luke.

'I couldn't agree with you more.' Bob added, 'In fact, it's a disgrace the place should have survived as long as it has.'

'And now a birth of community care, a better way of treatment, but a bad side to it nonetheless.'

'Yes, not cash but public reaction; a rat race for patients to be put back in; a life race. It's going to be so bloody hard for them. Still, it's a thousand times better than caging people'

Luke nodded. 'Anything resembling Rosedale needs to lie down, breathe its last and die.'

Although such a topic of talk would invariably absorb Doctor Driscoll who was fascinated by psychiatry's future, at the moment he was far more preoccupied with something else. For suddenly his conversational angle switched to complete optimism, but not, Luke felt, with sufficient realism. Luke listened as Bob seemed to somewhat monotonously ramble on about a mixture of quite unrelated, disconnected topics. Bob asked Luke if he thought that his life was one of more minuses than pluses, if his life was disproportionately a negative net balance.

To that, Luke carefully steered around the central issue of successfully forged and maintained relationships, in contrast to those broken and failed. Luke found his colleague fluctuating between hope and despair, but as soon as Luke broached Bob's inclination to bisexual affection, Bob seemed to quickly radiate brightness, an alacrity of optimism.

Bob said that the current hurricane in the psychiatric health service had, in many ways, done him a lot of personal favours, getting rid of callous colleagues and, most useful of all, now allowing him to treat Danny Broughton out in the community, no longer tied within the institution. Luke probed this, asking in what precise capacity treatment in an open setting for Danny made things so much improved for Bob.

What did Bob's rather narrow term of treatment imply and entail? Just clinical help and giving of medication, or just therapeutic chats, or something more? Luke wasn't stupid, he knew it was something more, and nothing to do with psychiatric treatment at all. It was an obsessional lust, one highly unprofessional, a desired homosexual affair, one-sided, fuelled entirely by Bob's sexual ambition, but assuaged of guilt in Bob's conscience, because Bob had deluded himself that such a relationship was in some crazy way therapeutic, of benefit to Danny Broughton.

Bob had actually successfully lied to himself and come to accept this as truth, justified by doctor–patient canons of clinical ethicality. Luke had for some time detected a core of considerable self-centredness in Bob: like Bob maybe never thinking of how poor Danny felt about it all. And indeed, as Danny's entries in the notebook all too clearly revealed, it was a totally one sided infatuation; one initiated by Bob and sustained unrealistically and totally unprofessionally by him. For instance, had Bob ever even remotely considered Danny's schizophrenia affliction with exclusive sympathy, which it should always have been professionally? Even ethically? Or was Bob's massive concern self professed in a dedication for Danny's body, not Danny's mind? Did Bob really wish to help a young mentally ill man, or simply touch and kiss his skin? Was it ostensibly a caring approach of clinically, highly dubious concern? Luke felt to his horror that this was unmistakably, terribly so.

How could a clever specialist of the human mind be so impervious to reason? How could Bob so blindly, without the slightest inkling, not realise that Danny felt no true love, but felt instead just a nervous, rather mixed up fear of Doctor Driscoll's power, his formidable presence. Had Bob never realised Danny's lack of spontaneous desire, an affection not reciprocated? Was the delusion, then, a huge blinkering of Bob's perception in a logical reasoned way of the truth? Was the disorder, Luke wondered, a narcissism of egocentrism, one which had reached such an advanced stage that now Bob's mind was incapable of conscious compromise, of reason, ultimately a possibility of a flight of power of a conscience?

Nobody on earth could convince him of Danny's real feelings towards him; he just blindly assumed a glorious upturn of fortune and happiness by way of a mass of dark hair currently resting upon a Rosedale sickbay pillow. Any temple area scar – a legacy of Drake's philistinism – didn't reduce Bob's fierce, unswaying desire at all; in fact it increased Bob's sense of commitment by having heightened his feelings of compassion.

In all this Luke was lost for useful intervention; he'd never felt so useless at trying to help another human being. And that was the rub, the tragic part of it all. Bob was still so irreducibly human. Despite his affliction, he was still Luke's best friend.

Luke felt so uncomfortably stupid in all his futile attempts to be of help. What could he do? Suddenly, he decided to take a bold jump right into the heart of it all, to tell Bob that a notebook might be agonizing reading, but it was something which couldn't be delayed any longer.

'It's in a drawer in my small metal office desk,' said Luke.

'Are you joining me to read its contents, or would you prefer if I read it alone?'

'Just you,' said Luke, handing Bob a key.

Bob smiled in a victoriously deluded sense, a triumph which only existed in his own mind.

'And I'm sure its contents will easily disprove all the inhibitions you've been mooting and suggesting to me this afternoon. No disrespect Luke, but in this one I'm in the know, in the right.'

Luke didn't reply or make any physical gesture to suggest otherwise; he just stared out at the daffodils, his face serious and sad. He was almost in tears as he thought of that desk drawer bombshell of a notebook awaiting its victim; a victim in the form of an already worn and torn, nearly broken man. Such a display of emotion by Luke was unusual, for invariably his control over his expression of feelings was impeccable. Such a blast, Luke was quite sure would do its ugliest of work, its cruellest devastation. It would all explode in just a few minutes, the time taken for a middle-aged, proudly, if pathetically, walking figure, to go across a Rosedale courtyard and down a couple of corridors into Luke's office. Perhaps for the very first time in his life Luke couldn't at all predict what damage would be done to Bob, the outcome of it all. This was a tragedy in the making.

As he sat there silently, Luke reflected upon the absence of any human fairness or justice in the world. Although always having been a strong atheist, he quietly muttered under his breath that if, just if, there existed a god or creator who possessed power to alleviate suffering and heal broken hearts and minds, could it possibly come to the fore now.

Bob Driscoll was marching purposefully down a corridor, head firmly held up with conviction, the smell of anaesthetics all pervasive, busy nurses rushing to and fro. Bob was more than ever awaiting a return of so long exiled, bright beacons of hope after so long a time, of grey, hopeless, crying skies of a life he had no choice to be born into. A disillusioning career, a wife he'd badly hurt, a life of so little accomplished of what he'd always wanted to do; a life meaningless now in retrospect unless a saviour in the shape of Danny Broughton stepped in.

Bob's triumph would be to see Danny smile, such an expression being to dispel all rainy skies and implement permanent light. Such brightness of sunshine would witness all the Doctor Drakes of this earth scuttling away into shadows of insignificance, to the backwater of purgatory, their rightful place.

Luke was still sitting deep in thought as Bob was entering the office to unlock that bottom drawer. Luke reflected upon a battery of insoluble problems, and with great concern about himself of late. His own state of mind. He wondered if he'd began to contract a kind of insecurity neurosis disorder, a state of anxiety and indecisiveness whilst having worked in this particular type of job. The ineffectual kind of attitude, a walking medical dictionary of talk, talk, talk, but no action, no powers of resolution, no conviction. All such undesirable facets were in strong contrast to his early days as a psychology student: a dogmatic, assertive, firm, hard-headed character; a person who always did things, never simply analysed them as he so theoretically and lamentably had done in recent years in his position as the clinical top grade Rosedale psychologist.

He posed a direct question to himself: had he succumbed to a malaise of the mind too? A departure from reality? Had the insular institutional Rosedale culture rendered him remote from and estranged from everyday social life and human goings on? Had his ivory tower become his own prison of a breeding ground for unrealism? Had he cut himself off, albeit unintentionally, from the real world? Then he suddenly had another remarkable flash of insight – not just for himself but for all people alive in the hectic maelstrom of the closing years of the twentieth century. It was a staggering revelation. Could it be, he wondered, that in modern society reality is too harmful, too dangerous and potentially damaging to a normal healthy human psyche; unable to be handled satisfactorily, so that only an abnormal unreal human attitude can win, can go with the flow? Does only the madman today, with an unreal perception and perspective, have the ability and success to survive and not flounder in a crazy unreal society?

Does one have to adopt or possess a mind of unrealism in order to cope with a modern ethos of unrealism? Luke then realised why he might personally be bordering on a mental disorder; he'd so commendably maintained his rationality and sense of balanced reason and had clashed with unreal, insane currents of a modern age so much so that he had developed a possible neurosis. His stance, so long adhered to, of rock-hard realism was the cause of a possible downfall due to undefeatable overwhelming odds, odds in the shape of an invincible, unreal modern age of thought.

He then, correctly but regrettably, deduced that if he was to avoid a mental demise he'd have to adopt a more unrealistic stance, an attitude more in harmony with the kind of modern world and its philosophy in which he had the misfortune to have to live. Only his outstanding insight was saving him, a faculty that Suzy or Bob Driscoll didn't possess. Unfortunately, Bob Driscoll might be too far on the road towards a breakdown which was incapable now of any attempt to put in reverse; a point already reached of no return. Certainly over the next few minutes such a speculation would be critically put to the test, a realization for Bob of infinite, priceless loss, a robbery of all his future possessions in the way of anything that mattered or was meaningful to him.

Hence, a demoralized Luke Lloyd Evans realized the irony of all ironies, that the most lethal therapy of all is not a surgeon's knife or an assault of electric shocks, but instead is the undeniable, unalterable triumph of misfortune and grief, not just in mental institutions but in the entire human world. A global affliction for those so wounded by life's brutal punches and kicks as to put such undeserved victims in comas brought on by trauma and distress. Almost a deathly sensation to have to feel: the paradox of a strange comfort, relief and rest when death does in fact eventually arrive.

The cruel joker in this random pack of unfair cards is that everyone is tragically led to expect a fair deal, a bit of sunshine for all individuals. Such expectations are lost in the darkness of grim facts of an unfair bargain, one where nobody had any real choice to enter into or any option to refuse. A compulsory game of frequent grief, a game called human existence. Indeed Bob Driscoll was finding that out right now as he picked up and opened a small, rather tatty notebook; such writings within pushing a destructive force through any remaining defenses he had to guard against an onset of insanity. Yet it was worse, not only a permanently contracted mental illness, but a spectre transcending his mortal existence; damnation, an eternal victim of fate.